LAKE EERIE

JOHN LEE SCHNEIDER

SEVEREDPRESS

LAKE EERIE

WWW.SEVEREDPRESS.COM
WWW.WILLIAMLONG.CO.UK

ISBN: 978-1-922861-26-9

"It is the thrashing struggle of distress that triggers the piranhas' natural instinct to target the weak and the helpless."

Jeremy Wade

CHAPTER 1

"Are they biting?"

Artie glanced down at his phone as the text announced itself with his wife's ringtone. The dim electric glow was bright as a lantern in the misty lake's bare predawn twilight.

He tapped a frowny-face symbol in reply.

Although *something* was biting – he just wasn't catching anything.

He had been standing hip-deep in the middle of the rapids for an hour and gotten no response at all, but that changed the moment the first rays of light touched the morning mist. Since then, he had already been through five leaders.

Whatever was out there, he was getting the first look. The lake had been closed to the public for years, and opening day of fishing season was still two days away.

Artie, however, believed in aces up your sleeves and head-starts.

Rumor was, this was a dead lake. It was already known to be a sequestered, isolated body of water whose native trout population had crashed, pressured by invasive catfish, among others. Fishing, as a sport, had been kept on a resuscitator for many years by a local hatchery,

The hatchery was quite popular, with sportsmen and conservationists alike. Its owner was an organic fish-farmer that specialized in restocking threatened or endangered freshwater species, who had settled on the lake in his retirement.

After he died, however, the facility fell into other managerial hands, who turned to more profitable genetic-modification methods – a fool's errand in the region, as they became the immediate target of activists, who shut the place down in less than two years.

One side-effect was the population of trout on the lake plummeted.

A moratorium on fishing was subsequently imposed, ostensibly to allow the trout time to recover, but worked more practically as a permanent ban, because there was no natural mechanism to bring them back. There was brief talk of restocking with farmed fish from other hatcheries, but that was also quickly snuffed over possible genetic modification.

After that, everything basically stayed in stasis, leaving the lake unused, stagnant and dead. The last Fish and Game report said that, after all these years, trout were as scarce as ever, and now the catfish seemed to be gone too.

But the moratorium was expiring. And they were letting the lake reopen anyway.

There had been some question whether the local academic-egghead advising Fish and Game might stand in the way – a third-wheel twerp, named Kenny Mitchell, who was barely out of high school when the moratorium was first imposed – but he let it pass.

"If people want to pay for a license to fish where there are no fish," this particular third-wheel was rumored to have said, "why not let them?"

Artie was of two minds there.

He *was* out here, after all.

First and foremost, these long-neglected lakes sometimes had little pockets of really nice, fully-grown fish – always provided you got to them early. And *that* was why he was out a couple days early, because he was *not*, in fact, going to pay to fish where there were no fish. He was testing the waters first.

Secondly, and probably more truthfully, he was out here because it had been too damn long.

Artie had spent a lot of time on this lake. It was his childhood *and* his youth, and he'd reached his middle-age waiting to fish it again.

So he would give it today. If the lake really was dead-water, he wouldn't have missed any of the official season, and could still be anywhere else on opening day.

So far, he wasn't sure of his answer, as he felt his line go limp once again.

Muttering curses, he began reeling in the slack.

He wondered what was doing it – the lake-bed was sharp lava that ate a lot of tackle, and the area was heavily forested, providing a lot of snagging branches, but this felt like a fish-hit – a tug and a pull – and it was taking the line in a single strike.

That might be a good sign – maybe these were just really BIG fish. It might even make the hazardous trip out here worthwhile.

And there *were* hazards. The lake lay at the center of a treacherous patch of wilderness – rough mountain terrain, cresting the Idaho side of the Washington border. You got bears, including grizzlies. It was also known for quicksand and sinkholes. Geothermal activity kicked up a tremor, now and again.

It went by the nickname, *'Lake Eerie'*. As if its official designation wasn't descriptive enough – the original settlers called it *'Lake Perdition'*, because of the constant layer of mist, like brimstone drifting up from the netherworld.

The lake was a conjoined series of rain and snow-filled lava pits. With constant geothermal pressure from below, pockets of steam regularly broke through, as underground heat forced its way up, mixing into the cold water and mountain air. The lake-floor was also brittle and prone to sinkholes, as the underlying crust broke away.

It was a large lake, running twenty-five miles, although it was narrow and broken by the rugged landmass into several distinct lochs, creating islands, pooling into various scattered coves, nooks and crannies, all through the surrounding mountains.

Once the sun burned away enough of the eldritch mist, Artie would have a nice view of the modest falls, which drained the rain and snow-melt from the surrounding peaks.

In the soupy semi-darkness, however, visibility was near zero.

But then, just as he blinked, Artie thought he saw a flash of light penetrate the mist.

He paused, peering into the murk. It looked like the light on a boat.

Artie frowned.

There was only one person he could think of who might actually be out on the lake this dreary morning, and that was a man known around these parts as Hayden Marshall Wyatt – spoken of formally by locals with his full proper name.

If there was a single person in the county Artie wanted to run into less than Hayden Marshall Wyatt, he couldn't say who it might be.

A more detestable fellow, Artie never met – always showing up out of nowhere, and causing other folks grief. He had not one single personable quality – he was cold, taciturn, rude, and generally unlikable.

Besides that, he was the game warden.

Artie watched for several minutes and saw no repeat of the flashing light.

Finally, he turned back to his tattered line. His count was six leaders now.

He glanced after the phantom light on the lake, grumbling. So far, all he was guilty of was littering the water with his tackle.

Sterner measures were clearly required. This time, he attached his lure to a twelve-inch length of wire – the sort of gear you normally used fishing for sharks.

Artie found himself considering freshwater bull sharks, often found in oddball lakes, far from the ocean.

He smiled, shaking his head. Besides being way too far north and more than a thousand miles from even the frigid Pacific Ocean, any possible connection to major rivers were several miles *down*stream.

But creepy thoughts like that occurred to you out here – it was called *Lake Eerie*, after all, and it was easy to let your imagination run away with you.

Artie tied the wire to the end of his line and cast back out.

To Hell with Hayden Marshall Wyatt – Artie knew he'd get busted whether he caught any fish or not, just for being out on the lake. Wyatt was the sort who'd arrest his own son if he ever met a woman sour enough to give him one.

There was an invisible splash somewhere far out, where his cast hit the water.

Artie waited a moment, listening to the sounds on the lake.

The falls, less than a quarter-mile away, were a steady murmur, like background traffic. The running water of the rapids masked any more subtle sounds.

That was another thing about Lake Eerie, it left you blind *and* deaf. Artie heard stories about bears walking right up on completely-oblivious fishermen over by the falls.

Of course, the falls were only one corner of the lake, and most fishing was done by boat – within season, that is.

Truthfully, Lake Perdition never really was a popular spot, even for those who liked rough wilderness. It was remote and difficult to access, with most of the lake properties accessible only by water.

It was also just a more-dangerous than average place to be.

Because of the direct snow-melt from the surrounding peaks, spots of the lake could be extremely cold, so simple water-activities like swimming were risky.

Worse, because the lake floor was both brittle and hollow, the steady, tumbling water of the falls created breakaway rocks. Combined with the shallow bottom and typically misty conditions, these just-under-the-surface rocks were quite a gauntlet for boats – the waterway surrounding the falls had earned the nickname *'Purgatory Cove'*.

Beneath the lake-floor was a catacombs of lava vents, flooded by thermal-heated ground-water. The periodic breaks in the basin, announced as this heat bubbled-up like a giant bullfrog, burping funnels of steam right out of the lake surface.

Groundwater broke through beyond the perimeters of the lake as well. A mile into the hills, beyond the northern bank, was a natural hot-springs – a small grove with steaming pools of water – a site that might have been an attraction except for being so remote – a hike that led over sharp

4

lava rock, often coated with invisible black ice, as the steam from the springs froze in the cold air.

The springs were also known to 'run hot' – depending on concurrent geothermal activity, the water-temperature could go scalding. It had happened in the months prior to the St. Helen's eruption, in 1980, and again right before the 1989 Los Angeles quake. People had been badly burned on both occasions.

That was not to mention those odd bears. Cougars, too. There had been more than one attack incident – no known fatalities, although people in the area did have a tendency to go missing and never be found.

Beyond the hot-springs was open wilderness. The peaks beyond Lake Perdition were the last place any human had any direct cause to go for hundreds of miles.

You could see why it might be a little too woodsy-wild for some.

Of course, the same had often been said about Artie himself.

Still, he didn't want to just waste his time. He checked his watch. It was still early. He would see how his reinforced leader performed. If things didn't change, he might just pack-up.

Artie knew the surrounding rivers were reported to be plentiful with big fat trout this year and he could fish any one of them with none of the risk, or sheer inconvenience.

But *something* had been biting, and stubbornness ran in his family. And as a lifetime fisherman, there was always that golden dream of that long-neglected patch, that dark cubbyhole, just waiting to reveal the biggest, plumpest fish he ever caught, grown fat, unmolested by fishermen for all those seasons.

Although to be truthful, that was his vision pretty much every time he fished.

As if on cue, Artie finally felt a real strike on the line.

This time, with the wire leader, the line held – he had something hooked.

And it felt *big*.

Now there was a sudden flurry of movement, jerking the pole in his hands.

"Whoa," he said aloud. "There we go!"

The violent tugs continued for maybe twenty seconds, pulling wildly in several directions.

Then just as suddenly, it fell heavy and dead.

Frowning, Artie began reeling-in, feeling something dragging along the bottom as he hauled his catch in over the rapids.

In the early-morning dimness, he could see a dark clump bumping along on the end of his line. As he pulled it in close, he realized it was a fish-head – behind the gills, it had been completely eaten away, bones and all.

Artie reeled it in, pulling it out of the water, holding the tattered head up to examine.

"What the *hell?*"

At first, he'd thought it was a large pike, or some other heavy-bodied fish, he'd never seen in the lake before.

Then he saw the teeth, and realized what he was looking at.

This was a piranha. And a pretty damn big one at that.

In Idaho.

Artie turned the dead fish on the line. The bites taken out of it were the size of golf balls. Bigger. Just in the few seconds that this fish had been on the line, it had been targeted.

By its fellows.

Artie blinked in realization as he looked down at the water around him, and then back at the cannibalized fish dangling on the end of his line – his first catch of the day.

And his last, he decided, as he pulled out his pocketknife to cut the fish-head loose.

As he did so, he saw another flash of light coming from the lake. It was closer this time – definitely a boat.

Wyatt, Artie thought. Had to be. Not but the very damn *second* he catches a fish.

Now a spotlight flashed through the fog and Artie heard the distinctive growling drawl that chilled the nerves of every outdoorsman in the county.

"Artie?" Hayden Marshall Wyatt called. "Is that you?"

With the instinctive panic of a kid caught with his hand in the cookie-jar, Artie swiped his blade across the line, and cut the incriminating fish-head loose, tossing it quickly in the water.

Almost instantly, something hit it from below – the impact was enough to kick up a splash of water.

In seconds, it was hit several more times.

Artie stepped back, stumbling briefly.

Then something hit his leg – a good heavy blow, like a large branch smacking against his shin in the rapids.

Less than a second later, he was hit again – multiple times. He looked down and saw black, darting shapes schooling in the churning water around him.

Artie realized the brine was clouding red with his own blood.

Gasping with sudden horror, he reeled backwards, stumbling towards shore.

He felt no pain, but as he looked down, he saw his leg was already laid open to the bone. He let loose a guttural and nearly-involuntary scream.

Wyatt's voice called over the water.

"*Jesus*, Artie! What the hell? Are you okay?"

There was the sound of a boat motor, turning towards the mouth of the rapids.

Artie screamed again, as he lunged for the bank, only to discover his legs no longer worked with all the muscle stripped away, and he fell face-forward.

Something hit him in the face like a fist the instant he hit the water. The blow was nearly heavy enough to knock him out – perhaps a blessing, as he stared, semi-dazed at the foot-long, black shapes mobbing in, teeth-first.

There was a fusillade of blows across his arms and legs, then his ribs and belly.

The rapids washed the water clear enough of his escaping lifeblood that, in his last moments, Artie could see what was happening to him.

He'd been gutted – hollowed-out – even before the oxygen had sufficiently faded from his brain to lose consciousness, he was already half-eaten.

Already dead.

His last thought, as the darkness clouded over his eyes, was that it didn't hurt a bit.

Artie's body continued to kick and toss in the water as the swarming fish stripped the remaining bits of flesh.

By the time the spotlight found his corpse, there was nothing left but gnawed skeleton and ragged clinging clothes. He still clung to his fishing pole with one hand.

Hayden Marshall Wyatt looked down at the minimal remains that had recently been Artie Langstrom. Then he reached a boat-hook over the side and fished him out, letting the skeletonized corpse fall to the floorboards. There wasn't even enough tissue left to bleed.

Wyatt frowned, running his finger over the dead wounds like he would a poached deer.

He shook his head, cranking his motor, as he turned the boat back out onto the lake.

CHAPTER 2

Sarah hadn't been out on Lake Perdition in twelve years. She never would have again but for a call from an old friend.

Adequate to the occasion, he asked her to come look at a dead body.

Sarah had known Kenny Mitchell since junior high. Now he was scientific adviser for the small local Fish and Game office.

He knew this would be personal to her.

"Sorry," he said. "But I had to get you in on this one."

He described the game warden's story in a few brief sentences.

There was an awkward moment of silence. Without further discussion, Sarah agreed to travel out that morning – an hour shuttle-flight, and another hour's drive in a rental.

It was still mid-morning, but the sun was making an atypically early appearance on the lake, burning through the clouds. The water, normally cloudy with mud and forest debris, was clear blue as the emerging sky above. It perpetrated the illusion of a beautiful, idyllic summertime lake.

But Sarah knew better – once, she had fallen for that cruel lie, but never again.

The man driving the boat glanced back.

"You okay, ma'am?" he asked, seeing the look on her face.

He had introduced himself simply as *Wyatt*, offering a brief pump-handshake, when he met her at the morgue that morning.

"You're the fish-lady? Mitchell said you were coming."

Fish-lady. Sarah's brow arched, but she nodded.

Kenny had warned her about Wyatt.

"He's a bit colorful," he said.

'*Colorful*' was not wrong – for the moment, they cruised in deliberate silence, as efforts at conversation had so far ranged from awkward to terse.

Sarah didn't know how to describe Hayden Marshall Wyatt, but she'd only known him a short time and was already sure she'd never forget him.

He had eyed her appraisingly, when he led her in to see the victim's body.

"Just so you know," he told her, "it's not a pretty sight."

"No need to be condescending," Sarah replied. "I'm a doctor."

Wyatt nodded.

8

"Yes, ma'am," he said. "And I was a Marine. And I'm just warning you, I puked in my mouth a little."

He pulled up the sheet, exposing the cadaver beneath.

Sarah, who was not a medical doctor, nor by any means a person accustomed to graphic forensic examination, certainly never took gross anatomy, and whose dissecting experience was mostly restricted to fish, took one look and gagged-up in her throat. She brought her hand to her mouth, tasting bile.

The worst part was the bits of tissue that were left between the bones – clinging bits of meat and tendon, all that would be left for the insects and worms.

It was not the first time she'd seen something like this.

'*Skeletonized*' was Kenny's description.

"You know what that means," he said.

They both knew. Kenny had been out there on the lake too, twelve years ago. And once you'd seen it, there wasn't any mistaking it when the cause of death was '*eaten by piranhas*'.

And this victim displayed golf-ball-sized bites – some larger than that.

That would implicate one particular species – *Serrasalmus rhombeus,* the red-eyed or black piranha. Excepting a few varied sub-species, it was the largest of the truly dangerous breeds.

And it just so happened they were once farmed right on this lake, not so far from where Sarah spent every summer until she was seventeen.

Her family's lake-house lay barely three miles further north from where they were now, nestled in a cove on the very last accessible shore, past even the hot-springs.

Sarah hadn't been home in a long time.

Home was the wrong word – it was their vacation house, where she once kept all her best memories.

It was hers now – it had been for two years, inherited from her parents – a transaction handled strictly through lawyers, who arranged for maintenance and upkeep, until she could sell – although moving property on Lake Eerie was like trying to sell swampland.

These days, her childhood happy-place was shrouded in scandal and death. Sarah was just seventeen back when it all happened, and like a young girl, she had run away.

She hadn't made it obvious – she was graduating high school, already on her way off to college – but she never came back to the lake-house again. And rarely to her home in the city.

When she'd gotten word her parents had died in a car wreck, she hadn't been home to visit in over a year.

"It'll be good to see you again," Kenny told her on the phone that morning. "Deb and I are looking forward to it."

"You two need to come out to the lake-house," Sarah offered, even as she couldn't help notice the deliberate mention of *Deb*.

Deb Brown, administrator of the local two-person Fish and Game office, was one of Sarah's pair of teen-era BFFs, and the girl Kenny immediately rebounded to, after it became apparent his affections for Sarah were not returned.

Sarah cringed, remembering Kenny's painfully-obvious crush, helplessly unreciprocated on her part.

"I'll be staying at the old house," she said, "I've got extra rooms."

"We might take you up on that," Kenny responded.

The deliberate *we*, again. Sarah sighed regretfully. It seemed silly after twelve years, but little bits of the past seemed to cling like that – you never forgot the puppy-love crushes.

For Sarah, it was the first time she'd had to reject the affections of a friend.

The friendship had not officially ended because of it – twelve years of e-mails – but it soured. Again, it wasn't obvious, being the end of their senior year and already going their separate ways. But they'd barely seen each other in the years since.

Of course, extenuating factors contributed as well.

Lake Perdition was never short of those. Sarah would not have scoffed over a curse on the place. As Wyatt took them past all her old childhood haunts, there was no nostalgia – more the creeping chill of a past finally coming back to claim her.

This was the most remote corner of the lake. Just ahead, was Devil's Island, which was really more a three-mile protrusion of volcanic rock. It used to be five-miles until a massive sinkhole dropped the surrounding banks, particularly its south shore, right into the lake. That stretch was nicknamed the *'Boneyard'*, after the groves of old trees that still grew through the waterline, many of them large enough to slalom a boat around.

But even that was dying. Sarah had seen several floating logs, including one entire tree, whose roots had just given up their grip on the lake-floor. It was an indication that the Boneyard was decaying – the old trees were collapsing, setting adrift, perhaps barely under the surface, just waiting for the unwary boater going a bit too fast over the already-misty lake.

And that was typically the *safe* route – the south was a more open expanse of water. To the north were the falls, and the infamous Purgatory Cove.

But now, as they approached the island, they saw they weren't the only boat on the lake this morning.

Sarah blinked in recognition.

"Is that the *water-taxi*?"

Wyatt nodded as an old-style stern-wheeler came into view, chugging from the south, cruising midstream in the deepest water, far out from the Boneyard.

"Old Norman fired it up about six months ago," he said. "Now that the lake's opening back up, there's a summer-camp being built. He's been taking the construction crews back-and-forth to town."

Norman had been the lake's official caretaker since time began. In the days of the hatchery, he also ran a ferry-service for its workers, as well as renting out for charters.

In recent years, Fish and Game basically paid him for maintenance on the few empty properties that still stood out on the lake.

Sarah had always liked Norman, despite his generally cantankerous demeanor.

Then she frowned as she remembered Kenny telling her Norman had recently picked-up an apprentice.

Wyatt pulled to one side, letting the larger boat pass.

Norman waved from the pilot's window. Wyatt waved back.

But Sarah's eyes were on the figure standing behind him – another person she'd not seen in twelve years, and *that* one was definitely ON-purpose.

In high school, Robbie Ray was the bad boy – Sarah's own helpless, mad-crush, who also just happened to be dating her *other* best friend, Danielle.

Danielle Taylor was always *the* popular girl in her little pond – cheerleader, student-council, prom queen, daughter of the town doctor – the one who most enjoyed baiting her daddy with her hooligan boyfriend.

But Sarah, the girl-scout, apparently had a thing for bad-boys too.

Typical teenage drama.

Unfortunately, after high school, Robbie lived up to typical bad-boy expectations. Most of his trouble came after Sarah left – Kenny and Deb both suggested it was *because* she left. There were fights, drunken nuisance-type stuff – pedestrian, but sufficient to get him in enough scrapes with the law to do a little time.

"He just got out," Kenny told Sarah. "He started working on the lake last week as part of a government program."

The water-taxi's horn blared, and Norman waved again as the ancient stern-wheeler pulled away.

"Where are they going?" Sarah asked.

"They probably just dropped-off the camp-workers, and headed back to town."

Sarah hadn't heard of any camp opening on the lake – a lift on the fishing ban hardly made the place a resort. She wondered where they managed to acquire property.

Wyatt steered back into the main channel. Sarah's eyes followed the departing stern-wheeler.

She couldn't tell if Robbie was looking back.

Sarah wondered if he recognized her. She had on a sun-hat, glasses, different hair.

Yeah, she sighed, he had probably seen her.

She dearly hoped he left it at that. The last thing she needed was to rattle *that* skeleton out of her closet.

Sarah shivered, despite the growing warmth of the sun. Something about this lake just brought out the chill in you.

Or maybe it was just *her* – too many ghosts – too many memories.

It was like that everywhere – they passed the old hatchery, several miles back, and its dark, boarded-up buildings seemed to loom like tombstones.

If a lake could be called a ghost-town, Lake Eerie was it.

The local town had never originally been given an official name – when founded, it sort of adopted the name *Perdition*, although the lake was named first. It was half bedroom-community for Lewiston, a hundred highway-miles south, and half low-income housing bordering the surrounding woods. The lake itself was another thirty miles out.

Sarah grew-up in Lewiston and only spent summers on the lake, but that was where she knew all her best friends – Kenny, Deb, Danielle, all lived in town, and Sarah couldn't wait to get out to the lake every summer, spring, and Christmas break.

But as an adult, she lived in Seattle. She hadn't been to the town of Perdition in years. Like the lake itself, it had gone to seed.

It was as if the ecological health of the entire region was failing.

The hatchery had fed more than the lake with fish. Besides its own modest workforce, which allowed a couple dozen families to live near the lake, it provided an industry – the influx of fish kept the lake stocked for fishermen, who in turn, rented boats and charters, bought bait and lures.

Leo Pike, the hatchery's owner, was a deceptively gentle man, who lived right across the cove from Sarah's own family lake-house. He had opened the hatchery in semi-retirement – a local rich-man's project, intended to do no more than stimulate the struggling indigenous trout population. But he was already widely-known and favored for his natural organic methods, and once he'd put the assembly-line in place, word-of-mouth brought demand for everything from fertilized eggs, to tankfuls of mature fish, to be released live.

And Sarah, as Wyatt had put it, had been a 'fish-lady' all her life. She was fascinated and a bit awed by Mr. Pike. His property, visible from her own window, was landscaped with elaborate koi-style ponds, filled with exotic species from all over the world.

From the time she was thirteen through high school, Sarah babysat for Mr. Pike's daughter, Lori, relishing any opportunity to be given the run of the wonderful, modern-Gothic house, and most especially, all its fantastic pools of otherworldly fish.

She had been there the night Mr. Pike had died.

Danielle Taylor had died there too.

And they died horribly.

When they were found, it was very much like what Sarah had seen at the morgue today.

As it happened, one of the exotic species Mr. Pike kept in his ponds was, in fact, *Serrasalmus rhombeus*, the Amazonian black piranha.

Apparently somehow, maybe even because of what happened that night, they had gotten into the lake.

But they still shouldn't be able to breed. The water was too cold. Piranha had been introduced into many American lakes and rivers, but never successfully.

Still, if somehow they *were*...?

It had been twelve-years.

They would have had time to *grow*.

"We're almost there," Wyatt announced abruptly, startling Sarah out of her reverie.

This was once considered the best fishing spot on the lake – an open expanse of water running between Devil's Island's north shore, and the rocks of Purgatory Cove.

The shallows were good for bugs and fish alike, as were the jagged, randomly-strewn rocks, lurking invisibly under the surface, abetted, as if with deliberate diabolical design, by the particular geography of the lake, so both the sun and the moon cast reflective mirrors over the surface – not to mention the constant whistling breeze that kept a camouflaging ripple on the water, masking anything that might be skulking about below.

Many boats had their underbellies gutted, gliding over hidden rocks – more than one at high-speed, completely misjudging depth near the falls and crashing with impact.

And as if accepting sacrifice, the lake claimed just a few more lives.

Sarah supposed every major lake must be like that – how many people died each year, recreating on the water? Fishing? Skiing? Swimming? It happened. There was no need to make it into more than it was.

But it *did* seem like a constant cloud loomed over Lake Perdition, figuratively and literally.

The settlers eschewed the place and passed it by – an oddity for a large body of water.

On the surface, it appeared to be the perfect, natural mountain lake. The deterioration into the dead place it had become, was usually cited as corresponding with the closure of the hatchery, but it really began two years before, when Mr. Pike died.

Sarah wished she could say that night had started out innocently. The truth was, her and a few friends were taking advantage of a babysitting-gig to party in a beach house.

At the time, there was a lot of rumor around town about what really happened that night.

For Sarah, things changed forever. Her coping method was to simply leave it all behind. She had no intent to change that – she was here to do a job, not exorcise personal demons or rattle skeletons in the closet.

Some of them might not be dead yet.

Sarah glanced back after the water-taxi, but the big stern-wheeler was already around the bend, out of sight.

CHAPTER 3

Norman and Robbie both stared after Wyatt's boat.

Wyatt, Norman thought bitterly. Boy, did he hate *that* sonofabitch – always showing up where he wasn't wanted, causing folks grief. Naturally, they had to cross paths *this* morning.

"Was that who I think it was with him?" Robbie asked.

Norman didn't answer – it wasn't a question.

He saw the look on the younger man's face and hoped he wasn't witnessing a setback. So-far, the kid had greeted the new job with enthusiasm, shaking off prison with an up-from-zero attitude. That was something that could carry you past a lot of trials as an ex-con.

Crashing hard over an old flame, on the other hand...?

In Robbie Ray's world, Sarah Campbell was his silver bullet.

Norman hadn't forgotten how it was to be young – he'd cracked a bottle or two over a lady in his day. He'd even had his own scrapes with the law.

Robbie was a smart kid, but he led with his heart. That had gotten more than one man into trouble.

Norman scowled after Wyatt's boat. It had been a good morning until now.

They'd just escorted the latest round of workers for that new summer camp. According to their five passengers – pretty, young, college-girls, except for a token young fellow who looked cookie-cut from some California surf-n-sun beach. This was their orientation week – the camp was about to open, and the kids would be arriving in two weeks.

"Troubled tweens," one of the girls explained to Norman. "Runaways, abuse cases, druggies."

The young woman introduced herself as Adrienne, batting her eyes earnestly – beauty-pageant/social-worker.

"I'm a counselor," she said, proudly.

"Of course, you are," Norman agreed, admiring her scantily-clad figure, dressed in anticipation of summer-lake weather.

For their part, Adrienne and the other girls – Amy, Anne, Dana, and Donna – all traded giggling glances at Robbie, posed up top, steering the boat. Robbie played it cool – the dark, smoldering desperado.

Jack, the displaced-surfer, was more concerned with the overcast sky and the definite mountain chill hanging in the air.

"Doesn't the sun ever come out?"

"It's like this every morning," Norman replied. He waved his hand at the moody cloud-cover. "This will burn off by midday. You'll get your sunshine."

Jack's face brightened. Settling back, he smiled invitingly at Adrienne, who returned it just as brightly, even as she kept one roving eye on Robbie.

Norm chuckled, thinking that it was good to be around people again.

They'd dropped the lot of them off at the campsite dock twenty minutes ago.

Once the property had been ol' Leo Pike's house, the same fellow who started up the old hatchery. His wayward daughter, Lori, still owned the place. In fact, as Norman recalled, she inherited a good amount of money after he died.

But she was only twelve years-old at the time. Rumor was, she had her own troubles – sent to live with an uncle, who had health problems and also subsequently died. Since then, she had been rampaging through the rich teen-age and young-adult club-scene over several states.

She'd blown her money in all the standard ways – drugs, booze, repeated rehab. Her last DUI made the news, after an all-too-brief but high-speed chase, and it appeared the authorities were losing patience with her.

The property on the lake was the last thing she owned, primarily because she hadn't been back since her father died. It was her one remaining asset to barter – the 'camp for troubled tweens' was an arrangement to keep her out of jail and satisfy community-service requirements.

Just like Robbie, Lori was getting a chance to set her life right. Those things were always a toss-up.

"She's back too," Norman informed Robbie as they neared the property. "She's living here now."

Robbie nodded and stayed discreetly in the pilothouse while they dropped their passengers off at the dock.

Norman remembered the scandal. Robbie was one of a bunch of teenagers partying it up at a beach-house on the lake. Two deaths were involved, both ruled accidents.

One of them was Lori's father, Mr. Pike.

The other was more personal to Robbie – a popular cheerleader Robbie dated for a year, who was not at *all* happy to discover he was sneaking around with her best friend. There were several people who testified to *that* – it had been a conversation held at high-volume.

What happened later that night was a bit of a gray area.

Most would-be witnesses, including Robbie himself, claimed to have been blackout drunk.

Robbie was still severely questioned by law-enforcement, and might have been a suspect had the whole incident not been simply declared an accident.

It followed him anyway. Funny thing, Norman thought – when people passed group-judgment, they tended to make sure you served the time as well. Robbie never went to jail for anything that happened *that* night, but he made it there anyway.

Now that he was out, he retreated to the lake.

But it seemed his past had come home as well.

Norman glanced at Robbie, who was still staring back where Wyatt had disappeared with Sarah.

That was Wyatt for you – stirring it up even when he wasn't trying to. Trouble seemed to waft off of him like the mist on the lake.

"I wonder what the sonofabitch is doing out here?" Norman asked aloud. "Trying to catch someone getting a jump on the season?"

Norman had been on the end of Wyatt's flashlight once, out on a neighboring lake many years ago. It was before Wyatt was even assigned Lake Perdition, but by reputation, the game warden was a boogeyman who could be on every mountain and every river in the region at once – and Norman wouldn't have been the one to say he wasn't.

"There was some kind of an accident this morning," Robbie said. "I saw it on the Lake's website." He held up his phone, showing the headline.

Norman, who had been given a two-thousand dollar iPhone by Fish and Game, and used it for nothing but direct person-to-person phone calls and had no e-mail, nodded.

"No wonder I didn't see it," he said, squinting at the tiny screen. "What happened?"

"Someone was killed out on the rapids. Some kind of animal attack."

"A bear?"

"It just says *animal attack*."

Norman frowned.

Lake Perdition was named after Hell. Maybe that had an effect on a place – bad karma or something, because it seemed like bad things happened here a little too often.

And every time it appeared things might be looking up, you got something like this.

Norman had watched over the lake for a long time. He'd been a charter-pilot, ran a twice-daily route as a ferryman – he was even licensed to carry postal freight.

These days, the job basically consisted of watching over old, empty lake-houses, mowing lawns, doing maintenance. He lived in an old lakeside cabin about five miles north of the public docks – living on a lake, and not even allowed to swim or fish, and boating for necessary-travel only.

Norman had been the only remaining person living out that far for several years, ever since his wife, Ethel, died.

He'd always been a bit reclusive, but seeing other people was something he hadn't realized how much he'd missed. It had been a treat to ferry the campsite construction workers over the last couple months, pulling the old stern-wheeler out for the first time in years. He'd even been getting calls about charters for opening day – old lake-property owners coming back after all this time, revisiting houses they had never been able to sell.

It was also nice having a new helper on board this week, someone to talk to. He'd been living isolated so long, he'd almost forgotten what it was like.

He hoped some stupid accident wasn't going to go and close it all up again.

"Some damned hiker," Norman grumbled. "Trying to feed a bear. It wouldn't be the first time."

But Robbie shook his head.

"If it was a bear attack, why did Wyatt have Sarah out here with him?"

"She's the college-wilderness-expert-type, right? Like that Mitchell-twerp back at the office?"

"Yeah," Robbie said. "But she studies *fish*."

Norman considered – bringing a fish-expert in on an animal-killing was not suggestive of a bear.

But Lake Perdition had other history as well.

Fish-attacks in American lakes were not unheard of – large sturgeon, catfish, and other large lake-fish were probably competitive with sharks for fatal attacks in the US, most often by dragging down fishermen or grabbing swimmers – although the cause-of-death was drowning as opposed to being bitten in half or eaten.

This would not be the first person killed by fish on Lake Perdition, either.

And last time, it had not been any catfish.

Norman exchanged a grim glance with Robbie, and they both looked back where Wyatt and Sarah had disappeared round the bend into Purgatory Cove.

CHAPTER 4

Wyatt guided them carefully past the falls over to the rapids where Artie Langstrom had been killed.

Sarah observed his careful, steady moves, each measured tap of the wheel as he threaded them past the jagged rocks, his face stern, brooking no distractions. Sarah remained dutifully silent, letting him navigate.

A lifelong academic, Sarah was not the biggest fan of either military or law-enforcement – in her world, both were violence, which she hated in all its forms. Necessity or not, the very nature of either profession inevitably attracted the thuggish.

Sarah hadn't made up her mind about Wyatt, but he came from both worlds, and word-of-mouth wasn't exactly fawning.

According to Kenny, Wyatt was assigned the territory just before the lake closed down, because Field and Game wanted someone who could keep a tight lid on the place.

Sarah could definitely see that in him.

Wyatt pointed to a split in the shore a quarter-mile past the falls, where the water grew shallow over cobbled lava-bed, and a small stream emptied into the lake.

"That's the spot," he said. "Artie was standing in the rapids when he got hit."

"You saw it?"

Wyatt shook his head.

"Fog's thick in the morning. Too heavy to see. But I heard splashing and I heard screams. And not much more than a minute after that, I pulled him out of the water. You saw yourself how he looked then."

The game-warden shook his head.

"Artie's not the first person we've lost out here this season," he said. "We always lose a *few* folks every year. But it's already been a bad one."

"What happened to the others?" Sarah asked. "How many are we talking about?"

"I don't know what happened to the rest of them," Wyatt replied. "Artie was the only one I was there for. The others just turned up missing. Maybe they all went this way."

"Who were they?"

"A couple groups of college kids. A few come up to the hot-springs. Pretty much the only thing that'll draw anyone out anymore. And that's illegal too."

"You never caught anybody out at the springs?"

Wyatt shrugged.

"I don't prioritize it. Despite what people say, I can't be everywhere. I'm not as concerned with soaking in a natural hot-tub, as I am poaching, be it illegal fishing or hunting." He nodded purposefully. "I don't miss many of those."

As a scientist, Sarah was tempted to ask exactly how he knew what he might have missed, but actually found herself inclined to take him at his word.

"The first two that went missing," Wyatt continued, "we found their backpacks floating out in the lake. No bites or torn clothes, or anything like that. And no bodies either. Just their bags floating in the middle of the lake.

"The others," he said, "the larger party, just disappeared. We never found anything. Seven missing, all told."

They certainly wouldn't be the first, Sarah thought, looking around at the surrounding mountains and heavy forest stretching for miles in every direction.

The hot-springs were not the only unique feature along the north shore. Just over the ridge, Sarah could see what looked like a rising pillar of smoke, but was actually billowing steam and water-vapor drawn from both the hot-springs and the lake itself.

Looming like a dark tower on the lake, this natural smokestack was nicknamed, 'the Cauldron'. It was the very tip of a modest peninsula, where the hillside had partially broken away from the main landmass, leaning askew like an Eiffel Tower, creating a narrow ravine between.

Along its base, on the beach below, the split in the rock also left a cave/tunnel leading through the outer cliff wall into a small, terrarium-like, hollow basin, that was heavily grown, and constantly filled like a cistern with rain and snow melt.

The broken and eroded wall was pock-marked with lava-vents, that channeled the mist from the lake like steam from a witch's brew.

These vents also turned the wind whistling through the Cauldron into notes on an instrument – low, haunting moans constantly echoed over the surface of the lake – and when the weather gusted-up, the wild screaming of a banshee

Or perhaps, on Lake Perdition, the wails of the damned.

And, boy, if *that* wouldn't raise the hair on your neck, those dark nights when the wind blew.

The Cauldron had been long-barred from public use. The cave leading from the beach to the modest courtyard was always sketchy with crumbling rock, and finally collapsed several years ago. Rather than clean it up, Fish and Game simply left it as a natural barrier to keep people out.

Now, the only way to access the Cauldron basin was with climbing gear. Of course, that was banned too, after one couple tried it, and fell into the water, which was usually nothing but freshly liquidized ice. They suffered hypothermia and drowned.

Another fellow attempted a free climb, clinging to the vegetation growing along the wall – which, as it turned out, wasn't quite capable of holding his weight. That gentleman landed on the rocks, broke his leg, and died of exposure after three days.

There were a number of other close-calls requiring rescue, and the Cauldron officially became one more place you couldn't go.

Eventually, people just stopped coming out to the lake at all.

The lake itself seemed to have gotten used to that. There was an isolated silence Sarah didn't remember from the old days.

Even the mist seemed heavier than she remembered. It *had* been a heavier than average snow-year. The hot-springs got a lot of the spring-melt, and when that ice-water hit those heated pools, you could see the steam rise from the hillside like an eruption, always with a secondary spout funneled through the Cauldron.

It all contributed to higher humidity, clouds, and the generally overcast, supernatural gloom that loomed over the region. The lake was surrounded by places called Hoo Doo Canyon, Dead-Man's Pass, all heavily forested and blanketed in a constant lurking fog – perfect for a Gothic castle in Transylvania, and every bit as isolated.

As a kid, it had been her backyard.

Barely a mile further along, nestled along the bank of the last major inlet on the lake, was Sarah's own little cove, and the lake house that was now hers. Growing-up, she could see the smoke of the Cauldron from her bedroom, the constant billowing mist, mysterious and mystical.

The little cistern that had formed in the Cauldron's pit was sometimes called the *'Ninth Level of Hell'* – one of ice, because people trapped in the collected pool of mountain rain and snow-melt usually froze to death.

Sarah herself had fallen-in once as a teen. She had grown-up scaling every sheer rock and cliff around the lake, but on this occasion, she'd been working without a harness and her grip on the rope slipped halfway down, dropping her almost fifty feet – *luckily* – into the middle of the collected pool of ice-liquid instead of the rocks.

But the water had been *cold* – it literally sucked her breath away.

"Oh my GOD," she had gasped, struggling to the surface, floundering for the surrounding rocks. Her teeth chattering, her hands going numb, she had barely managed to pull herself out, even as Kenny and Deb hollered down after her.

The Cauldron was just one example of the churning volcanic landscape. The entire area was a labyrinth of connecting tunnels under both the mountains and the lake itself, some flooded with groundwater, others with molten rock – occasionally, these mixed.

Besides the decades-old example of the Boneyard, smaller sinkholes continued to open up periodically, over random parts of the lake, often taking down whole trees – some of these were actually sucked down into the flowing subterranean ground water and spit back out miles away. Animals had likewise been trapped and drowned – the odd deer or moose had been discovered floating the same way.

Lake Eerie was just a damned hazardous place. And it had *way* too many skeletons in the closet.

Sarah could easily imagine ghosts dancing in the last of the morning mist as it wafted off the lake's surface. She found herself thinking of her parents, two years gone, now.

"Ma'am?" Wyatt said abruptly, interrupting her thought.

Sarah started to attention.

Wyatt brought the boat to a stop just short of the rapids. The water was shallow but clear, meaning you could *see* the gauntlet of sharp rocks just waiting to tear out the floorboards – which was a sight better than *not* seeing them.

"Right here," Wyatt said. "Maybe half-hour after sunrise."

"Was he injured?" Sarah asked. "A wounded or struggling animal is one of the primary stimulus that activates swarming attacks. *Something* must have triggered it."

"Ma'am, I have no idea. I spotted his boat tied-up in the brush, and I figured he was getting a jump on the season. But like I told you, I couldn't see through the fog."

"You didn't shoot him and then he fell in, or anything like that?"

Wyatt frowned.

"No, ma'am."

His eyes narrowed and Sarah thought he was getting ready to be angry at her, but instead he took a deep breath.

"Listen. In two days, this lake's about to open up for fishing for the first time in twelve years. I need to know if I have to postpone or delay that. I've already posted word of this incident online. But some folks are already going to be out on the water or camped-out. That gives me twenty-five miles of lake to cover."

He eyed her seriously.

"It's just me out here. If I have to close it up, I need to know why. Is it the ecology, or is it safety? Is it a few days postponed, or completely closing the lake? Again?

"These," he said, "are things I need to know. And quickly."

Sarah nodded, although she knew he wouldn't like her answer – because what response could she really give?

As an academic, Sarah would have downplayed the danger posed by piranha. Except pesky reality kept imposing itself, contradicting printed literature.

In their native environment, risk was situational. However, when certain conditions were met, piranha could be extremely dangerous, famously known to 'skeletonize a cow in less than a minute'.

And could they *really?*

Absolutely. If there were enough of them, especially, large adults.

More importantly, w*ould* they?

That answer was the most basic of all – how *hungry* were they?

Sarah had found that piranha were one of those species where all the experts seemed very protective, quick to dispel 'man-eating myths'. Shark-experts were the same way.

And Sarah would be fine with that except that they were just as quick to insert their own mythology about that same fish's benevolence. And while that might be beneficial to the fish, it could end up being quite harmful to a person who believed it.

It seemed ridiculous to have to say it, but *yes*, piranha *were*, in fact, a fierce, aggressive, and dangerous fish.

Most animals with bad reputations did something to earn it. While it was true they were not deliberately evil, demonic beings targeting humans out of malice, but rather simply behaving according to instinct, that still might leave a person dead, and sometimes eaten.

Certain animals *were* flat-out dangerous. Fossil-records show big cats always hunted humans, given the opportunity – they didn't need to *'learn'* man-killing, although many picked-it-up once they discovered how easy humans were to kill. Crocodiles were also extremely dangerous, utterly amoral, and would aggressively prey on humans with impunity.

Danger from sharks varied widely with the conditions and species. At one time, people were commonly eaten by the hundreds after shipwrecks. And you wouldn't want to be swimming around the Farallon Islands during seal season.

Piranha also had conditional triggers, and at times, they might seem very stand-offish. But that could change in a heartbeat. It was worth remembering that almost *all* fish were predators – even plant-eating species were known to turn predatory.

Sarah had seen one recent study actually describe piranha as *'timid'*, and *'not true predators'*, because they were, in fact, omnivores.

What *'omnivore'* meant was that scientists sometimes found up to twelve-percent plant-matter in piranha-bellies – the reason being, because they were so voracious, they literally ate anything in front of them, like razor-toothed, underwater locusts.

'Timid' referred to the tendency, as a smaller fish on the Amazon – a river rife with caiman, giant armored catfish, and a multitude of other carnivorous denizens – for piranha to shoal together when confronted by predators – exactly the circumstance under which they might launch a swarming frenzy. Because there were only two – hunger and a threat.

They were fish – their behavior was not complicated.

And as fish go, they *were* quite pugnacious by nature – you couldn't put them in a tank with other fish, even other piranha, because they were so aggressive. Sarah had one at the Institute that attacked its own reflection so repeatedly, it cracked the glass of its tank, splitting its own face, leaving a snarling scar between its nostrils.

There were communities living on the Amazon where the average person was missing a finger or toe – cited in that same study as evidence of non-aggression because of a low fatality-rate.

Of course, that was *recorded* fatalities. Because of the very rural nature of these communities, most fatal incidents were anecdotal.

But as the eyes and cameras of the modern world penetrated ever deeper into previously unknown territories, a lot of supposedly discredited *'myths'* were proving painfully true. Piranha *would* attack a live person in open water, no different than any other animal – they just had to perceive that hint of distress, just like the chemical signal that caused a hive of bees to attack.

Today, it had happened right here on Lake Perdition, over five-thousand miles from the Amazon.

Sarah looked into the clear, shallow water, and saw no darting trout, no catfish, but no clutter, either – the lake seemed remarkably clear.

"The foreheads back at the station say they haven't been catching anything," Wyatt remarked. "They were still getting trout for a while, and then catfish. But lately, nothing." He shook his head. "No piranha, either, though."

Sarah nodded. The 'foreheads' would have been Fish and Game officials, Kenny and Deb, when they came out twice a year, for population samples.

"Well," she said, "you won't be catching piranha if you brought tackle for trout or catfish. They'd bite right through that."

Piranha-jaws were among the most efficient biting mechanisms ever designed by nature, proportionately exceeding the P.S.I. of Great White sharks, crocodiles, or *T. rex.* They had tightly-packed, interlocking teeth, designed for rapid puncture and shearing, taking cup-shaped bites out of prey – mounted on the end of a short, squat body built for repeated high-velocity impact.

Those jaws could easily explain why no one had caught any until now. Lake Perdition was known for eating tackle, and fishermen had taken to lighter-strength line that would break away, rather than wrestling the rocks and branches for their tangled lures. A piranha would simply bite through the line, and the angler would never know what they'd hooked.

But Sarah came prepared. From her pack, she produced her fishing rod – an expensive, heavy-duty spinning-reel rod, designed for feisty fish. She assembled it quickly and attached a ten-inch strip of wire to the hook above the lure.

"You know," Wyatt said, "it's a thousand-dollar fine for fishing out of season."

Sarah paused as he stared at her, absolutely deadpan.

Then he shrugged.

"That was a joke," he said, without smiling.

Sarah stared back, doubtful.

"Really," he said. "It's okay. I'm officially giving you permission."

Sarah nodded, neutrally – that remark had not helped.

She put the rod to her shoulder and cast into the middle of the lake. There was a splash fifty-yards out and she immediately began to reel in the line, keeping the shiny lure bumping close to the surface.

Almost immediately, the line was hit.

"*Whoa,*" Sarah said, brows raised, as she felt the powerful tug. "This is something heavy."

She could see the dark shape in the clear water and knew what she had even before she hauled the battling fish in.

There was a thump against the hull as it turned and charged the boat, just before Sarah pulled it up and out of the water.

Several other dark shapes darted briefly below the boat, only to disappear immediately, once the struggling fish was pulled out of reach.

Sarah deftly turned and dropped her catch into the boat.

"That," Wyatt remarked respectfully, "is no little fish."

Sarah pinned the creature to the boat-seat, running a tape-measure from head to tail. It read sixteen inches. She guessed it weighed more than seven pounds.

"This," Sarah said, "is a very *large* black piranha."

The fish kicked, the vicious jaws snapping for her hands – she jerked her fingers out of reach.

Wyatt made the point moot a moment later, as he whacked the fish stiffly across the head with a boat-hook. Sarah let out a brief startled screech, as the fish quivered and went still. She blinked up at Wyatt, who was looking at her mildly.

"You weren't planning on throwing that back, were you?"

"Well," Sarah said. "Actually, I don't usually kill what I fish for."

Wyatt shrugged.

"Well," he said, "we'll call this a sample-specimen for the other eggheads."

Sarah's eyes narrowed, but she let it pass.

She looked down at the fish staring at her with its dead eyes.

Piranha had such mindless eyes – programmed for nothing but aggression.

Sarah looked around at the surrounding water. She'd caught this thing on her first cast.

"Well," she said, "that's it. They're here. And you've got a problem."

CHAPTER 5

For a week, Lori had stood in the background of her own house, watching strangers buzz about, pounding away at the final renovations before the camp opened. Now the construction crew was gone and the actual councilors were due to arrive that very morning.

The rest of the minimal staff was already in place. Dave Nelson, the administrator – and in recent months, Lori's latest assigned handler – had been onsite, overseeing the construction.

The other two were waiting for Lori as she trundled into her kitchen, looking for coffee.

"Good morning, sunshine," a bright, if gravelly voice greeted.

Henry, the camp-cook, was sitting at the breakfast table, with his wife, Pamela.

Lori smiled at the old couple.

Henry had worked for her father at the hatchery back in the old days. He had already been at the house for a few weeks, cooking for the construction crew. His wife, Pamela, a former RN, was brought in as housekeeper/nurse.

"The wife likes it," Henry said, when Lori first arrived. "We're both retired. The work's light and we get to live on the lake for a few weeks."

A nice retirement job, Lori agreed. In her own case, the camp was the offer she had been given by the District Attorney's office – part of the deal her father's lawyers had settled-on.

Ironic, that after twelve-years, she still thought of them as her father's lawyers. And they were still managing her affairs.

The main building was still technically her house, but the senior-staff, Dave, Henry and Pamela, would stay in the guestrooms during the season. The house would be otherwise empty during the year, during which, Lori's 'job' would be off-season maintenance and upkeep.

The small-print of *that* little clause dictated that she 'maintain her presence at the site'.

Translation: *you don't leave.*

As part of her community service, Lori would also be required to tell her own story as a troubled-tween (and beyond) – tales involving a lot of booze, drugs, and highlighting with at least one on-camera car-chase –

basically, regurgitating and reliving a lot of high-profile events she would rather forget.

Lori knew to count her blessings, but *that* was why she was less enthusiastic about being back at the old family house.

"You'll do fine, honey," Pamela assured her, handing Lori a cup of coffee.

Outside, they heard Dave calling out a greeting to the water-taxi that was now arriving at the dock.

Lori had met Dave only a few months ago, right after this camp-project was announced, assigned by her father's lawyers to 'help her oversee the project' Basically, he was her new babysitter, and was already living onsite when Lori arrived. He greeted her with an appropriately-firm handshake, piping near-constant motivational-jargon, so excruciatingly positive and upbeat, it *had* to be an act. Lori was only waiting for him to show up drunk at her room some dark night.

As the water-taxi docked, Lori recognized old Norman waiting behind the railing with a mooring line.

"Who's driving the boat?" Lori asked.

"I hear Norman has a new helper," Henry remarked.

Pamela gave her husband a severe frown, swatting at his hand, spilling his hot coffee.

"Owww, *bitch!*" he yelped. She rapped him again smartly, on the cheek, holding her hand up to her lips for silence.

Lori looked out at the arriving boat and its passengers.

Then her eyes found the figure standing discreetly in the pilot house. It was a face Lori knew well – a little older, a little darker under the eyes.

She had *such* a crush on Robbie back in the day.

But she hadn't seen him since the morning after.

Lori remembered Sarah holding her back. There were police and emergency choppers. And after it was all over, Lori had been taken away.

She had never seen her father, except for something they carried on a stretcher under a sheet.

It was later reported that 'all the teenagers on the scene were being questioned by authorities'. She also heard 'Robbie Ray' mentioned repeatedly as a 'person of interest'.

Of course, they were all eventually cleared – or more properly, the entire incident determined to be unfortunate happenstance.

But the investigation had taken weeks, and Lori wasn't sure anyone really knew for sure, one way or another.

Dave greeted each councilor with his appropriate-handshake as they exited the boat. Lori gave them all a quick once-over – four sorority-girls and a frat-boy, education or social-services majors – all dressed in beach-wear and looking a little chilled in the morning dank.

The camp itself was ready to go. The main house was already large, intended to house staff and guests, and needed few renovations.

Out on the grounds, her father's ponds were torn up to make way for the two single-story dorms, designed to resemble old-style boat houses, rustic-looking but solar-heated – one for the councilors, one for the troubled-tweens.

Outside, Dave was giving his orientation tour.

"Are there boats?" Jack, the frat-boy asked. "I was told there were boats."

"We have boats," Dave assured him. "We have canoes, rubber-rafts. We also have two speedboats for water-skiing and inner-tubing."

Dave checked his watch.

"We'll be going until about two-o'clock today. After that, you can get out on the lake if you want."

Jack winked a wolfish eye at Adrienne and Dana. "You with me, ladies?"

"Be careful out there," Dave cautioned. He indicated the sun and deceptively blue sky above. "The morning mist burns off, but it builds up again pretty quickly at night. It can leave you blind. And keep south of Devil's Island, away from Purgatory Cove."

The troop of them passed briefly out of sight, as Dave led them around the front. The door rattled and Lori sat passively as the group of strangers was now led into her house. Introductions passed to Henry, then Pamela.

Lori shook each of their hands dutifully, offering a minimal 'Hello, nice-to-meet-you', before Dave led them on to the laundry, kitchen, and living room.

"Chin up, girl," Henry offered. "This is a good thing you're doing here. Whether you're being *forced* to do it or not. You might as well embrace it."

Lori considered. That was actually a better pitch than she'd gotten from her lawyers – or any of her *own* councilors, for that matter.

Henry's eyes followed Adrienne and Dana's bikini-draped glutes.

"Yes," he repeated whimsically. "A *very* good thing."

Pamela swatted him smartly on the head.

"Owww," he muttered. "*Bitch!*"

Lori smiled, ducking out onto the porch as the old couple fell to squabbling.

It was, at least, a beautiful day – rare this early in the season. Hopefully, that bode well for the reopening. The lake could stand a few good omens.

She walked out to the dock, looking after the water-taxi as it rolled slowly away.

Then her eye turned across the cove, to the single property on the other side, another dwelling that had been empty for a long time.

Lori shut her eyes, almost physically pushing old memories away. Today was about starting over, not digging up old graves.

Wasn't that what all her councilors kept hitting her with? Letting go of the past?

The truth was, Lori was actually fine with that. She always had been. That had never been her problem.

She glanced after the departing water-taxi.

The problem was when the past wouldn't let go of you.

CHAPTER 6

By two-o'clock, the sun reached its high point and it finally felt like summer.

In the open expanse of water south of Devil's Island, the drone of a speedboat sounded for the first time in twelve-years, as Jack came zigzagging on water-skis, with Adrienne and Dana at the wheel. The sounds of their laughter carried across the water.

Below the surface, the growling engine echoed across the basin and at the sudden approach of the large, threatening shape, the piranha shoaled together.

It was a large school, two-hundred or better – a shimmering cloud, moving quickly, just under the surface.

Contrary to popular belief, shoaling was a defensive response, not hunting behavior – piranha were most formidable in numbers, so when threatened, they gathered together in force.

The hot-dogging ski-boat charging upon them fast certainly seemed threatening enough. These fish hadn't seen many boats beyond the big stern-wheeler that had been lumbering up and down the past few weeks, or the odd forest-service boat.

But this was *loud* – noisy – intrusive.

It was also approaching from the deeper water, leaving no escape route, trapping the shoal against the rocks.

As the boat drew near, the congested mob scrambled, like tapping on a fish-tank.

They retreated into the Boneyard, but the ski-boat turned and followed them into the grove of dead and dying trees, weaving between them. Jack began doing full-body flips, showboating as near to the half-sunken trunks as he could.

Dana rolled her eyes.

"You know this guy's a moron, right?"

"Yeah," Adrienne agreed, smiling, "but he's gorgeous. And I'm only here for a few weeks. This is my summer."

Jack grinned broadly, skiing one-handed, waving the girls faster. Instead, Adrienne zigzagged, almost cracking him up. Dana laughed.

"Almost got him that time."

Jack adjusted his grip, settling down onto two skis.

As he did so, he caught a glimpse of a large mass floating on the water.

It was the carcass of what looked like a moose, caught between the trunks of two trees.

Dana and Adrienne had already motored by and missed it, but Jack could see the thing was stripped to the bone.

He got a good look as he was towed past. It was not decayed – the scraps of tissue still clinging to the bone were fresh.

Then something hit his ski, small and heavy, like tripping over a rock - it was enough to topple him, and he tumbled face first into the water.

"Uh oh," Dana said, looking back. "He's down."

Adrienne glanced back, arcing the boat back around the trees.

Behind them, there was splashing, as Jack seemed to struggle.

The moment he hit the water, the response from below was instantaneous – a surge, as dark shapes came swarming with explosive, eye-blinking speed.

And these fish were *big*.

Most cases of mass-attacks by piranha involved 'red-bellied' piranha – *Pygocentrus nattereri*. Smaller and more prone to shoaling, red-bellies were the species specifically referenced as 'skeletonizing a cow in under a minute'.

And those were the *little* ones.

Black piranha were not nearly so congested in their native environment – they lived on open moving rivers and had natural predators. Here, unmolested, they had time to *grow* – some were over sixteen-inches long, and the majority were at least a foot.

And now, after living undisturbed their whole lives, for the second time in a day, a motorboat invaded their home.

Fish had limited responses – in the case of piranha, it was defensive, predatory, and pissed-off.

Unless it was mating season – in which case, add gasoline to all three.

All Jack knew was, he was getting the shit kicked out of him.

He'd gotten beaten-up one time, over a girl in high school, by several guys at once. He was knocked-down and then kicked from every direction, helpless, on all fours, absorbing blows.

This was like that – he was aware of impact more than pain as circular-chunks, ranging from the size of a tablespoon to a pool ball, were chopped from his flesh in machine-gun succession.

The water was already turning red.

Jack grunted as he felt tugging at his hands and legs, severing tendons, stripping muscle – very quickly, he was left unable to swim, and his head dropped beneath the surface. Only then, when he saw the mobbing shapes, in the blood-clouded water, did he finally understand what was happening to him.

As they came, he waved his hand reflexively – *stop!* – and saw his forearm already gnawed down to the bone – he recognized the ulna and humerus from his high school anatomy chart.

Then he felt a barrage of blows on his belly. He lost his wind in an explosion of bubbles. When he'd been beaten-up that day, after it was over, he'd collapsed, gasping for breath.

Today, he couldn't breathe because he was underwater. Then he realized it didn't matter, anyway, because his lungs were already eaten out of his chest.

Now they came for his face. He blinked as a perfect circle of triangle teeth hit him in the cheek like a baseball-pitch. The impact knocked him dizzy.

In quick succession, he was struck in his face and neck.

As his life-blood filled the water in a red haze, Jack's eyes began to flutter – there was a tickle as he felt them moving inside his ribs, digging after his guts.

Jack's world finally faded to black. His life-jacket kept him at the surface, and his corpse continued to twitch and jerk, splashing water, but it was mostly over.

It might be debatable whether piranha could really consume a six-hundred pound cow in sixty-seconds, but two-hundred and fifteen pound Jack Burrell took easily under a minute.

During that time, Adrienne circled the boat around the grove, towards the spot they'd seen him splashing.

Dana leaned over the railing.

"Where is he? It looked like he was in trouble."

Adrienne slowed the motor, her smile fading. She stood, looking around.

"Maybe he hit his head," Dana ventured.

Adrienne nodded.

"Okay," she said, reaching for the railing, "take the wheel. I'm going down looking for him."

She started to climb over the edge, but Dana put a hand on her shoulder.

"Wait," she said, pointing. "Look."

Floating a short distance away, caught in the low-hanging branches, they could see the bright yellow of Jack's life-jacket.

"It must have come loose when he fell," Dana said.

Adrienne jumped back behind the wheel, restarting the motor, and turning them quickly around. As they drew close, Dana reached over the side for the floating jacket.

It was half-a-second before she realized he was still in it.

Or at least, what was left of him.

Dana sucked a huge, horrified breath, dropping the thing that had been Jack Burrell back in the water, and then exhaling in a loud, bugling scream.

"*Jesus!*" Adrienne hissed as she turned and saw the floating corpse, staring back with the empty sockets of its eyes, its face eaten away.

"My *God*," Dana gagged, one hand over her mouth. "What *happened* to him?"

"I don't know, but help me get him on board."

"Are you *kidding?*" Dana blanched. "I'm not touching... *that!*"

Adrienne rolled her eyes.

"Fine. *I'll* grab him. Steer us in close."

"I don't know how to drive a boat."

"Just like a car. Shift into reverse and back up slow."

Muttering, Dana briefly revved the motor too hard, before shifting into neutral and then into reverse. With a jerk, they began to troll backwards.

Adrienne reached over the side, grabbing Jack by the life-jacket, avoiding touching *him*.

The skin that was left was the worst part – bits of clinging meat, a few strips of hair.

At least he wasn't heavy.

Adrienne grabbed the base of his jacket to haul him up.

There was an immediate flash of movement from below. Adrienne jerked back with a screech, as the water exploded just beneath the surface, and something started tearing at what was left of Jack's corpse.

Dana responded with her own shriek and gunned the motor.

The boat lurched forward, nearly toppling Adrienne over the side. She grabbed the railing, and made a move for the wheel, but it was too late.

Their boat launched like a rocket, twenty yards, straight into the trunk of a large tree.

The two women were thrown forward, roughly. Dana smacked her head against the boat's windshield. Adrienne was knocked to the floor and her nose came up bloody.

Worse, as she rose to her knees, she realized the bottom of the boat was filling with water. The impact had ruptured the hull.

They were sinking.

CHAPTER 7

It was late afternoon when Wyatt turned their little boat into the final, most remote corner of the lake, an isolated little gully, barely three-quarters-of-a-mile across, the last cove with an accessible shore.

Sarah took a breath, bracing for the sight of it.

As they rounded the bend, the first thing she saw was the house on the opposite shore, once the home of Leo Pike – now, apparently, the site of a soon-to-open summer-camp.

Directly opposite the cove, tucked in a secluded lagoon all its own, was Sarah's old family summer home.

They were the only two private residences left this far out, and the legal wrangling over it had heated-up recently.

Idaho's Field and Game lawyers recently pounced on Lori Pike's legal and financial troubles to try and simply seize her land, on the grounds that she was irresponsible and couldn't be trusted to live in an environmentally-fragile area.

As a fellow property-owner, Sarah had signed a couple supportive documents via her own lawyers on Lori's behalf. It seemed the least she could do – it was certainly not out of any concern with keeping her own lake-house, or even losing the value of it, but she owed it to Lori. Sarah was babysitting the night her father died – you could make the case, Lori's life got broken on *her* watch.

From what Sarah understood now, after a quick call to her own lawyer, Lori nearly lost the property, and the counseling camp was the condition on which she kept it.

It had been that close. Sarah might have been left as last home-owner on the lake. What would have happened next? Would they have simply forced her out too?

The thought bothered her – not because she was ever there, but the idea the government could – and *would* – simply seize private property in the name of conservation. That not only locked the public out of the wilderness, but more to Sarah's distaste, it meant locking people *in* the cities – those over-populated cesspools that were the *worst* thing for the species *or* the environment.

On the other hand, Sarah fully intended to be shut of the property after her current business on the lake was concluded. When she'd heard the lake was finally opening again, her first thought was that the old house might actually sell now.

Because if there was one thing her trip today had clearly demonstrated, the lake's ghosts were still very alive in her heart. It was just a bad place for her now.

She'd already gotten feelers from her lawyers that 'conservation interests' might be interested in buying. Sarah had no doubt, if she sold, the old lake-house would quickly transfer into public-hands.

Better than simply being *seized*, she supposed.

Although, that would put the onus back on Lori, as the last property-holder. Sarah wondered if she would fight it again.

Wyatt turned into the lagoon and now the old lake-house finally came into view.

After twelve-years, Sarah's first impression was, it was like seeing someone who had grown long-hair and a beard – the trees and bushes around the place were all overgrown. Even the lily pads that once circled just the old boat-ramp, now covered half the lagoon.

The house seemed to sleep – or rather, hibernate. Norman had been diligent about his maintenance. The roof and siding were well-kept and the heavily-grown brush was trimmed.

But the house had an empty look, desolate and abandoned.

Patiently waiting, with a whole *cast* of ghosts from the past.

Wyatt puttered-up to the modest pier. He tied-off the boat and extended a helping-hand for Sarah.

Sarah repressed an impatient sigh – as if she couldn't climb a ladder to her own house by herself – but she took his offered hand and pulled herself up onto the dock.

Then he handed her the dead piranha she had caught, holding the seven-pound fish up by the tail.

Not exactly a bouquet of roses, Sarah thought, but accepted the carcass without comment.

"I'll pick you up here tomorrow at dawn," Wyatt said, in the manner of a man issuing instructions he expected to be followed. "That's 6:30. Sharp."

Then he paused, listening. With the boat motor turned off, they heard music drifting from the opposite side of the cove.

Wyatt glanced over his shoulder.

"I've been keeping an eye on that place," he said. "The construction crew has been there the past few weeks.

"The music," Wyatt said, "just started since Miss Pike has been back."

He nodded across the cove.

"We may have to speak with her tomorrow," he said. "As I understand it, there was a fatal incident involving piranha – specifically *black* piranha – on her property, about a dozen years ago. Seems to me, if we're looking for where these things might have come from, that'd be a good place to start."

Sarah perked an eyebrow. Wyatt knew more than he had let on.

"She would have been a child at the time," she said.

Wyatt nodded. "Twelve, about to turn thirteen."

He eyed her directly.

"I was also told," he said, "by Mr. Mitchell, our science-adviser, that you would be the one to talk to about it."

His eyes were suddenly watchful, and Sarah now realized he must already know about all the events at the Pike-house twelve-years ago. For some reason he had chosen to ambush her with it.

She wasn't sure why – just to see her reaction?

"I was there," Sarah said.

"I can't help but wonder why you haven't mentioned that until now."

"I've been thinking Mr. Pike's place would have to be the obvious first-source for this introduced population," Sarah replied. "But I can't figure out how they could have proliferated in these numbers. And why they seem to be behaving on the upper-threshold of the species' typical aggression? I honestly don't know, yet. I haven't gotten a look at the different areas of the lake. I was waiting to speculate until I saw more.

"And," she said, eyeing him directly, "if my personal business becomes relevant, I'll let you know."

Wyatt regarded her noncommittally.

"Fair enough," he allowed.

He looked back over the water.

"So, realistically," he said, "what kind of danger-level are we talking?"

"Well," Sarah said, "people work, travel, and fish in waters thick with piranhas every day. Attacks are rare in their native habitat. But they *do* happen. Certain conditions will make them more aggressive.

"On December 21st, 2005," she said, "at the end of Brazil's dry-season, eight people were attacked on a popular lake. Over the next seven months that same year, a hundred and ninety people were bitten."

Sarah shrugged.

"These were all individual bites," she said. "Which can be nasty. But they were not mass attacks, primarily because the fish were not gathered in the concentrated numbers necessary to create a true feeding-frenzy. In fact, it's believed the majority of the bites that year were from protective parents. Piranha are very aggressive guarding their nests.

"Those beach incidents," she explained, "were all minor injuries because piranha mate in pairs, and tend to spread out, so that level of aggression is not usually associated with the numbers you see in large shoals.

"It *was*, however," Sarah said grimly, "a different story in 1976, when a bus ran off a bridge into the Amazon River."

Wyatt nodded. "I read about that one."

"Thirty-nine passengers were trapped and eaten by piranhas," Sarah said. "Some drowned first, but others were undoubtedly eaten alive. Family members identified victims by their clothing."

Sarah had seen photographs of the dead. But while the images were gory enough, it was always the *thought* that made her shudder. It was bad enough to be bitten in half by a shark, but devoured one small bite at a time...?

The fleshless faces in those old Polaroids seemed frozen in outrage over the horrible way the fates had chosen for them to die.

"That," Sarah said, "was one of the worst incidents involving piranha that can be confirmed. But people travel that same river every day. They fish and swim."

"So what was the difference?" Wyatt asked.

"The people in the bus were probably panicking, struggling for their lives. That's just the sort of thrashing struggle that triggers the piranhas' instinct to attack. And once they get started, anything in their way is likely to get hit. Especially, in the close quarters of that bus.

"But," Sarah cautioned, "that was just one particularly horrific example."

She looked out on the lake.

"On the Amazon, it's the sort of thing that happens once in a while. Like a plane wreck. And when it does, there's no particular reason to attribute greater risk, because the piranha are *always* there."

Sarah shrugged.

"Based on that logic, it's tempting to say that, because attacks are rare where piranha have always been, they should be even *more* rare here."

She shook her head.

"But that's their natural environment. You could also argue that, because extreme conditions instigate attacks, their very presence on this lake already indicates a freak occurrence.

"You could even infer by the literature," she said, "it might actually be a *good* thing that we seem to be dealing with the largest species of piranha. According to academia, black piranha have less of a tendency towards shoaling."

Sarah waved an admonishing finger.

"I had an instructor who personally showed me footage of shoaling *Serrasalmus rhombeus* attacking a capybara. They have same shoaling-instinct all piranhas do. But black piranha are larger than the red-bellies, so it takes more to activate the threat response.

"There is also the fact," Sarah continued, "that this lake is a finite environment. On the Amazon, the constant movement of the river keeps the fish spread out. That's why the dry season makes them dangerous, when the water levels get low, and piranha get trapped in slow, stagnant ponds. Once they eat up everything – once they get *hungry* – venturing into their water is practically guaranteeing an attack."

Sarah waved a hand over the surrounding expanse of water.

"This lake has been closed for years," she said. "An entire generation has grown to full-maturity. In a complete absence of natural predators. *And* they have somehow managed to reproduce, which should not be possible at the average temperature of this lake. Acclimated or not, they simply are not evolved for it."

Wyatt nodded agreeably.

"Well, they're sure out here," he said. "I guess, this is one of those times science is wrong."

"It means there's something we don't understand," Sarah corrected. "Because they haven't just survived, they've *thrived*." She held up the dead seven-pounder. "This fish right here is the largest piranha I've ever seen. And that was on my first cast. I doubt I caught the king of the lake."

Sarah shook her head.

"A fish this size would require near-ideal conditions. They don't have that here."

"Well, ma'am," Wyatt said, "in my experience, nature finds her way around obstacles all the time. It's up to smart folks like you to concern yourselves with *how*. Guys like me gotta deal with it on the ground. So the bottom-line is, they're here, there's a lot of them. They're aggressive and big, and a potential danger to the public."

Sarah shrugged and nodded.

Wyatt sighed.

"Well that's it, I guess. I'm putting the season on hold." He shook his head regretfully. "I'm about to piss-off a *whole* lot of people."

He pulled out his phone, opened-up the lake's official website, and began to tap. He smiled as he hit send.

"Give it ten minutes before I'm getting cussed-out in the comments."

Wyatt turned towards his boat.

"Any idea what we need to be looking for tomorrow?"

Sarah pointed over his shoulder, where the steam billowing through the chambers of the Cauldron trailed into the air like smoke.

"A source of heat," she said. "There's geothermal activity all around. There must be a few pockets breaking through."

Wyatt nodded. He tapped his watch as he climbed into his boat.

"See you tomorrow. Six-thirty-sharp."

He tossed-off the mooring and cranked the motor.

Sarah watched him go. He had brought her all the way from town, twenty-five miles by boat. She wondered if he was going all the way back, or going to sleep on his boat?

Out on the water, the evening mist was already starting to form just above the surface. Wyatt's boat was already indistinct. He motored out into the middle of the cove, pausing, as if listening to the music coming from the new campsite across the way.

Then he turned towards the main lake and disappeared into the mist.

CHAPTER 8

Sarah stood at the end of her dock, and cast a hooked-lure out into the lagoon. The sun was just dipping over the western hills, and she wanted to take advantage of the fading light. Piranha were sight-feeders that slept at night.

As the lure and hook hit the water, she thought of Wyatt's thousand-dollar fine, and wondered if he would actually write it up.

Probably, she thought, as she began to reel back quickly, keeping the lure close to the surface. At the rapids, she'd gotten a hit on her first cast.

This time, however, there was nothing.

Sarah reeled the lure quickly past the surrounding moat of lilies. She cast out again and still got nothing. Then a third time.

Nothing. Sarah supposed that that should be encouraging. At least, they weren't everywhere.

On the other hand, according to her post-grad professor, who had done a lot of fishing on the Amazon, piranha were either feeding with a vengeance or not at all.

Sarah glanced up at the setting sun. It might simply be too late.

It was also particularly cold on her little corner of the lake, taking a lot of snow melt. Not that it should be a lot different from the rapids, just a few miles down.

So what *was* different? Different enough not just for them to be there, but to instigate such high-level aggression?

And if shoaling was defensive behavior, why would it be more prevalent for black piranha *here* than in their native habitat?

After all, the Amazon was positively wrought with deadly dangers, *mythical* dangers – the dinner-plate-sized wandering-spiders that spawned 'deadly tarantula' legends – large, highly aggressive vipers, giant anacondas, caimans *and* crocodiles.

That was not to mention a whole variety of less-publicized underwater denizens that were quite deadly in their own right – there were formidable giant armored catfish, and the diminutive *Candiru Picu* which would bore into you like a slithering, worm-like power-drill.

There were also river dolphins and giant otters, that fed on piranha with impunity.

Nor was the Amazon short of *human* fishermen, who were just as happy to catch piranha as any other fish.

If all that didn't goose black piranha into a defensive shoal, why now? Just conditioning? They'd never seen boats before?

Generally speaking, in their native habitat, there were two times a year that piranha became dangerous – one was the end of the dry season when the rivers ran low, trapping them in isolated lakes and ponds. Once they devoured everything edible and began to starve, anything that entered the water would be targeted.

Then there was mating season. That had been the presumed reason for the attacks in 2009.

Sarah had read the local ecology reports Kenny e-mailed over, running down the checklist defining the criteria for lifting the fishing moratorium.

One was that the invasive catfish seemed to have disappeared.

Sarah figured they could mark that box as mystery-solved.

Water-purity of the lake was also way up.

Ironically, the piranha were likely contributing to that as well. Rain and snow melt were purifying elements, but even normal levels of algae and bacteria were down – conditions normally created by the erosion of organic matter.

These sorts of natural pollutants were heavy in the swampy Amazon River, which was why that environment needed omnivorous swimming garbage buckets of the type that piranha had evolved into. Adding them to a comparatively clean northern lake like Perdition was like having snails in a fish-tank.

That would also explain the unnatural sparkle Sarah had noticed on the surface of the water today – the lake was clear as crystal.

If what *that* implied was true, they had reached a very dangerous point.

The size of the fish she had caught today suggested a very well-fed population – and gosh-be-darned if there weren't damn few trout left on this lake, and even the invasive catfish seemed to be mostly gone. So now, these fully-grown, gluttonous piranha-fish were eating random debris right out of the water.

They were hungry. Perhaps starving. In a finite environment.

Although, she thought, looking back out on her own lagoon, they weren't biting here.

So what was different from the rapids?

Accepting the fact that the lake itself was already cold enough to be barely livable, let alone breed, the simple geometry of her own lagoon should be *more* suitable, where the underwater plant stems, reaching into the lake floor, would mimic the plant stalks piranhas needed to lay their eggs.

Lily pads were always thick near the shore, packed together like a solid surface. When Sarah was a kid, their family dog, apparently seeing the clustered lilies as solid ground, stepped out of their boat, and dunked herself right into the lagoon, coming up startled and sputtering.

Sarah looked thoughtfully down at the lilies. Then she bent to her tackle-box, retrieving a pair of shears. Climbing down the side of the dock, she reached under one of the floating pads – cautiously, remembering the body she'd seen at the morgue – and she deftly cut the lily at its stalk and pulled it up out of the water.

As she examined the cut stem, she saw mounds of dead, rotting eggs gelled onto the stalks.

Sarah looked out on her little lagoon.

The fish *had* been there – they *had* tried.

It gave her a little shudder to think of them laying a brood under her own cabin, right beneath her feet.

But it was too cold.

Still, they were breeding somewhere.

Her eyes turned up the hill to the smoke from the Cauldron, funneled from the hot springs. The area was heavy with thermal – the heat was there. They just had to find it.

Sarah went inside and started pulling up temperature records online.

She sat at her father's old desk. Inside, the house was almost exactly the same. Besides yard maintenance, Norman brought in a house-cleaning crew every month.

But you could tell it had been shut a long time – it had that *smell*.

Somehow, it also seemed *dark,* even with the lights on, as if the lampshades had aged, and the electric bulbs had all dimmed.

Sarah's parents hadn't spent much time here in recent years. No doubt it had lost its charm for them as well.

She felt a brief pang of still-healing grief – she hadn't seen her parents in so long when she'd gotten word they died.

A sting of tears touched her eyes and she quickly blinked them away, turning her attention to the task in front of her – her professors called it 'work-ethic', but it was really more an emotional coping-method, which paid-off in academia.

Once she got lost in her own focus, it might be hours before her attention wavered. Tonight, she was finally distracted by noise coming from the opposite side of the cove.

Sarah opened the kitchen window, letting in the late-spring chill. The music coming from the campsite three-quarters of a mile away was loud enough to hear the words.

Lori was theoretically back as part of rehab. Sarah hoped the music wasn't a bad sign.

Wyatt mentioned the crew of college-age councilors had arrived at the camp-site today. They had enough company for a party.

Sarah wondered if she would see Lori this trip, or what they might have to say to each other.

She shut the window and closed the curtains.

But then, just as she sat back down, she heard a distinct *thump* – this time, from outside her backdoor.

That was the one off-note about the cabin when she was a kid. You *would* sometimes get the creeps out there all alone. The difference between being there with her parents, versus the few occasions they left her by herself, was more than night and day.

Although, night was definitely a good deal worse. The heckling calls of wildcats and birds were blood-curdlers.

But those were just sounds – the possibility of the odd bear could not be discounted. Or cougar. Sarah understood they were reintroducing wolves – not *native* wolves, because they were extinct, but larger timber wolves were apparently close enough.

You were also on your own if any unsavory *human* might come calling.

Sarah sat, listening for a repeat of the sound.

The only way onto the property was over the mountain and hundreds of miles of wilderness, or by the lake itself.

Keeping to the shadows, she looked out the window and saw a strange boat tied at her dock.

Someone was walking around to the front door.

Sarah's blood suddenly went chilled.

Robbie? Had he seen her, after all?

Twelve-years ago, she'd put a restraining-order against him, but that was long-since expired. She'd felt safe enough living in different states.

Not so much tonight.

Was Robbie the type who might skulk around her property in the dark?

Sarah thought he might just be.

He was the bad-boy, after all. Wasn't that what attracted her back when she was a stupid teenager, full of popping hormones?

What would she do if it *was* him? And what might his intentions be? Or... what if it *wasn't* him?

Sarah's father kept an old hunting rifle in a locked cabinet. Sarah had no idea where he kept the key.

LAKE EERIE

She did, however, have a good-sized cutlery knife, which she snatched out of the kitchen drawer.

Outside, the steps stopped halfway around the back deck.

Sarah debated just throwing the bolt-lock, but then looked around at all the open, scenic, lake-view windows. If someone wanted in, there was no need to come through the door.

Her heart pounding, she turned on the deck-light, and opened the door.

Outside, her porch was empty – the lamplight reflected back in the drifting mist.

Darkness there and nothing more.

And then a voice spoke up behind her.

"*Sarah!*"

Sarah screamed, turning around, whipping the knife in front of her.

"Holy *shit!*" Kenny yelped, nearly tripping over Deb as he stumbled back.

"Oh my *God*," Sarah said, even as relief washed over her. "I am *so* sorry."

Deb pushed Kenny off of her.

"It's okay," she said, archly. "You can jab him, if you want."

Sarah stood there a moment in the doorway, holding her knife, the three of them staring back at each other.

Then she started to laugh, opening her arms as Deb stepped in for a hug. Kenny joined hesitantly as Sarah threw her knife-hand over his shoulder.

"It's good to see you, Sarah," Deb said. "Sorry if we scared you."

Kenny tapped the cutlery knife dangling next to his ear.

"Scared *her?*" he said.

"Sorry," Sarah said, pulling back, opening the door behind her. "I was zoning on the computer. Come in."

Kenny grabbed up their overnight bag, glancing back where the music from the other side of the cove was reaching a crescendo.

"I take it you know who else is back?" he asked, as Sarah closed the door behind them, shutting the music off.

Sarah sighed, as she led them into the living room.

"Yeah. I heard she's had some troubles."

Kenny took the couch. Deb followed Sarah into the kitchen and produced a bottle of wine. Sarah handed her a corkscrew.

"For what it's worth," Kenny said, "I think she's been slapped awake, and she's really trying to straighten her life out."

"I wouldn't know," Sarah replied. "She just sort of dropped off my radar. She stopped texting me. Her email went dead."

46

"Shame can make people run and hide," Deb said. "A lot of times, from the very people that would help them."

Sarah shrugged.

"I don't know if that was me," she said regretfully. "Nothing would have happened that night, if I'd been being responsible."

Deb swatted her lightly on the head.

"Don't say that. It wasn't like you threw a party." Deb glanced furtively at Kenny. "I mean we all just sort of showed-up. We were kids."

"So was Danielle," Sarah said bitterly.

The three of them hung in brief silence. Deb poured three glasses of wine.

"I knew we were going to need this tonight," she said.

Sarah hesitated before taking her glass. She had an early morning, and no doubt Wyatt would show-up at six-thirty on the dot.

She had also brought up Danielle cold-sober – she wasn't sure she wanted to have that conversation with a loosened tongue.

"You've been blaming yourself for a long time, Sarah," Kenny said. "You've got to let it go."

"He's right," Deb said. "I mean, what good does it do?"

She shrugged, eyeing Sarah earnestly.

"And frankly, not to speak ill of the dead, but at some point, you gotta ask yourself, how much time is it really worth?"

Kenny nodded.

"Let's face it," he said, "Danielle was easy on the eyes. Most of us guys in school had a crush on her. But she wasn't always the nicest about it. I asked her to the eighth-grade dance. First girl I ever asked out. She told me she would rather go with someone else or by herself."

Deb nodded.

"Don't forget the part where she let you walk down the hall with your fly open after gym class, that same day."

Kenny glanced at her sideways. Deb smiled sweetly.

"You can't entirely blame Danielle," Sarah said. "Sometimes being pretty means unwanted attention. Sometimes *scary* attention."

Deb nodded knowingly.

"I guess Kenny told you. Robbie's out."

"I know," Sarah said. "I saw him today. Driving the water-taxi."

"A government program," Kenny said. "Helping old Norman on the lake."

"He got in trouble after you left," Deb said. "You might blame yourself for everything that happened, but folks around town blamed him."

"It was an accident," Sarah said.

"Well," Deb said, "at one point, he *was* a suspect."

"At one point, we *all* were."

"Yeah," Deb said, "but he *really* was."

"What does that mean?" Sarah asked crossly. "An extra-suspicious suspect in an accident?"

"You're defending him again," Deb said.

"No... I just... *Ughhhh!*"

Sarah threw up her hands.

"It doesn't matter. I'm glad he's out, but we're long-since over. We should never have been at all. That was how everything started."

An uncomfortable silence settled between them. Sarah felt a bitter note of melancholy – they'd been good friends back in school, but they'd barely seen each other in over a decade.

And people, Sarah knew, dealt with things differently.

They had never really talked about that night. After it all happened, Sarah had been gone.

Which really meant, Sarah had never talked about it with *anybody*.

Another reason to be careful with the wine. No need to be releasing inhibitions, enabling a conversation she didn't want.

Or an unsolicited trip down memory-lane to a night that changed her life forever.

CHAPTER 9

It was a starry night twelve-years ago – rare on Lake Perdition, a product of a northerly wind. And while the crispy breeze might have dispersed the mist, it lent an extra octave to the chimes echoing through the vents of the Cauldron.

Lake Eerie was particularly thick with restless spirits that day.

Sarah often babysat for Lori Pike during summers. Although technically retired, her father still worked odd, often late hours, sometimes traveling overnight. This time, it was supposed to just be a day-trip to Seattle, but it was already growing late when he called to report traffic was delayed by a bad car-wreck that closed the pass. He was going to have to get a motel, and asked if Sarah wouldn't mind staying the night.

Sarah had stayed over before. She was a regular visitor, anyway, as Mr. Pike had taken her under his wing as junior-protégé, and often had her at the house to look at his aquarium-quality fish gardens – Sarah could stare at them for hours.

Of course, young Lori was just as infatuated with Sarah, who was classically attractive, the way a budding tween, popping with young-adolescent hormones, couldn't *wait* to be.

To Sarah's amusement, Lori had recently entered a new phase – pushing thirteen and indignant at the idea of a 'babysitter', she started calling her evenings with Sarah '*girls' nights*'.

Sarah couldn't help but admire the younger girl's boundless confidence. According to Mr. Pike, Lori's first words were, "I can do it myself!"

That was a trait she clearly got from her father. Years later, as Sarah pursued her ichthyology-studies, she would draw upon Leo Pike's unique approach to his fish-farming, so different from the stale orthodoxy she was fed in academia.

"Genetic modification," Mr. Pike told her, "is Control-freak-101. What you *should* do is figure out how nature wants it done and do it that way."

Sarah often said, during her years at the university, a couple days a week walking with Mr. Pike through his fish-gardens beat *any* degree – simple things like monitoring temperature, stress-levels, even going so far as to play music, all resulting in a remarkably strong, healthy and natural population.

He kept a variety of exotic species. Besides the typical carp and koi, he had a big pond for sturgeon, and several species of very large catfish – massive, prehistoric-looking beasts with trailing, snake-like whiskers. There was even a turtle pool.

And in one of the ponds, carefully sequestered from the rest, were Amazonian black piranha.

"I like catfish for their whiskers," Mr. Pike told Sarah. "I like sturgeon because they're big. I like koi because their beautiful.

"And," he said, grinning, "I like *piranha* because they're *scary*."

He picked up a bucket of scraps – butcher's throwaways

"Want to see something?" he asked, tossing the first pieces of meat into the pond.

Instantly, the water came alive, churning to a boil, as the squat, muscular fish, that had been drifting lazily and aimless, suddenly launched headlong, attacking maniacally, each taking a chomping-bite and retreating, making way for the next. The goblets that hit the water were devoured in seconds.

"Here," Mr. Pike said, handing Sarah the bucket.

Sarah tossed the remainder of the scraps into the pond. When the last of it was gone, the fervor abruptly ceased and the water went calm, like shutting off a motor.

"I've always wanted to buy a cow carcass," Mr. Pike said, "just to see if they can really skeletonize it in one minute."

"Why," Sarah asked, "is a cow always the unit of measurement for such experiments?"

Mr. Pike laughed.

"I think Roosevelt's the reason for that. When he was traveling the Amazon, one of the native villages set up a little demonstration, damming off the river for several days, starving the piranha that lived there. Then they walked a cow into the water and let it be devoured alive."

A fairly callous act of cruelty, Sarah thought.

Still, she was curious.

"Did it take a minute?" she asked.

Mr. Pike shrugged. "I don't know if he had a stop-watch."

He indicated the pond in front of them.

"Actually," he said, "this little group of guys might take a while to eat a whole cow. A *big* group of black piranha this size, or even a good-sized shoal of fully-grown red-bellies? Well, that might be close. Within minutes, for sure.

"But," he said, holding up a cautionary finger, "that was a manufactured incident, not a natural event. They specifically created conditions to make the piranhas dangerous."

Now he stepped up to the edge of the pond.

"Here," he said, "watch this."

As Sarah watched, wide-eyed, Mr. Pike kicked off his shoes, peeled his shirt, and stepped into the pond.

The piranha, which only moments before had been tearing at the dead animal flesh in a frenzy, parted passively, as Mr. Pike settled down to his shoulders.

"See?" he said. "They're not being aggressive."

He paddled around briefly, for demonstration – moving deliberately smooth and slow, Sarah noted – before retreating back to the edge and climbing out.

"They don't normally attack animals larger than they are unless they're starving," he explained. "*Or* they pick up signs of distress."

He indicated the pond.

"Now don't *you* go trying that. These responses can change in a heartbeat. If I had fallen in and acted like I couldn't swim, or while they were still feeding, their response might have been very different. So, do as I say, not as I do."

"*Not* a problem," Sarah agreed readily.

The outdoor habitat was another example of Mr. Pike's methods. It would not normally be possible to keep such tropical fish outdoors, but he accessed a natural well on his property into his garden, creating a reservoir of thermal-heated water that fed the ponds. He also had solar-powered regulators keeping the temperature *just* right.

"It still took a few generations to build sufficient resistance to the cold," Mr. Pike said.

"Hybridized?" Sarah asked.

"No. Simply conditioned. Partly, it was the behavior of the fish themselves, adapting to their environment. Their mating-season altered, according to the local rainy season. They began shoaling together more than was usually the case in their native habitat – usually in the morning sunshine, hovering near the surface, possibly absorbing the warmth and using group-endothermy to move about in water that piranha might normally be stuporous. Or even dead."

"What if they get out into the lake?" Sarah had asked.

Mr. Pike had shaken his head confidently.

"They still couldn't live on the lake," he said. "At least not to breed. And a finite population like I have here, spread across twenty-five miles of lake? It's possible that some of them might survive individually, but they would simply live out their lifespan and die."

But Sarah had pointed to his own geothermally-heated ponds.

"Don't vents like this warm the lake?"

"Yes," he acknowledged. "In spots. But you have to remember that for the region, it's the difference between winter cold with snow-melt in the spring, and normal summer-lake temperatures which would still be in the fifties.

"Piranha," he assured her, "have never been successfully introduced into a North American waterway."

"Haven't they been caught in American lakes?"

"Individuals that have been caught were probably released pets," he replied. "Small enough to still be landed with normal tackle, and aggressive enough to bite at anything. They actually tend to get themselves fished-out because they beat the local fish to the hook."

The difference in the water-temperature was evident at night – the steam that formed on the lake became a virtual fog-bank over the ponds, and the house seemed to glow as the yard lights reflected the billowing vapor.

On cold nights, looking out the windows of the Pike-house was like being in a plane flying through a cloud. Combine that with a few animal cries and a good shrill waling coming out of the Cauldron, the house could get damned spooky after dark.

That was why on sleepovers, Sarah usually arranged for someone, usually Deb, to stay over with her. But tonight had been short-notice.

She also had to break a date.

And to shame the Devil, the truth was, she was a bit grateful for that part.

Kenny Mitchell had been her friend since Junior High, but just last week, he'd finally worked-up the nerve to ask her out.

Sarah's initial instinct was simply 'no' – but she was torn on how to handle it – she could hurt him by turning him down, or be nice and go on the date, which would just draw it out.

There was, however, a prickly situation that had developed.

It was called 'her best friend's boyfriend'.

Indiscretions, they might be called – maybe a dalliance or two – and they had started six-months ago.

Sarah knew she needed to stop herself, so when Kenny asked her out, she agreed – in retrospect, perhaps a selfish move. She was glad she'd been *legitimately* forced to cancel – hearing the disappointment in his voice was enough. There was no need to reschedule and repeat the mistake.

But for tonight, she was settled-up with blankets and popcorn, watching a scary movie with Lori – the original *Halloween*. And despite her protests of maturity, Lori latched onto Sarah like a spider-monkey every time the masked-boogeyman appeared on-screen. Later, it would be a *Friday the 13th* marathon.

They were both startled by a knock on the glass door to the back porch. They turned to see a silhouette outlined against the curtains.

"Sarah..." Lori whispered aghast.

But Sarah stood, walking over cautiously, peering outside. Then she pulled the curtain back and turned on the light.

Robbie started at the sudden glare.

"You *bastard*," Sarah blurted. "You scared me."

Robbie smiled.

"Like you didn't know it was me."

Behind her, Lori, not yet thirteen, but hormones percolating, stood at attention – she liked Robbie.

"Where can I get one?" she'd asked Sarah the first night he'd come over.

Robbie smiled at Sarah, leaning in the doorway.

"So," he said, "like some company?"

Sarah frowned.

"You shouldn't be here. What about Danielle?"

"She gave me a night out with the boys," he said. "I decided to come here instead."

"We're watching scary movies," Lori announced. "You can watch them with us."

Robbie grinned. Sarah sighed.

"Okay," she said. "Come in." She eyed him sternly. "But don't get any ideas."

Lori's presence would work as a chaperon for a while, but eventually, she would have to go to bed. That's how it happened last time.

It didn't help that Lori was nodding and winking every time she caught Sarah's eye.

And sure enough, once they settled down on the couch, and the *Friday the 13th* series began to roll, Sarah felt Robbie's hand slip around her shoulders. Worse, she found herself snuggling agreeably right under his arm.

He had just started to nuzzle her neck when there was another knock at the back porch.

Sarah sat bolt upright, pushing Robbie away.

Lori, who had been rapt on the TV as a hockey-faced madman chopped yet another victim, started to her feet.

Frowning back at Robbie, Sarah pulled back the curtain, switching on the porch light.

Standing outside, with big grins, were Deb and Kenny. Deb was carrying a fifth of Jack Daniels. Kenny had a case of beer.

"*Surprise!*" Deb announced, letting herself in. "Kenny said you were staying over, and I know you don't like to be out here alone."

Lori came running up excitedly to greet Deb, nodding dismissively at Kenny.

In the living room, Robbie stood from the couch.

Deb's eyes widened.

"Uh oh," she muttered, eyeing Sarah meaningfully. "*Busted.*"

At first, Sarah thought she meant the recently stood-up Kenny, but then she saw Danielle standing behind the others, holding their overnight bags.

Danielle's hot, fiery eyes met Sarah's briefly, before locking like a missile on Robbie.

"*Oh* uh," Lori echoed. "*Busted.*"

They all stared at each other in awkward silence.

The moment was broken as Sarah's phone rang in her pocket.

"Oh my God," Sarah breathed, looking at Lori, "it's your father."

She held up her hand to the others, who fell into dutiful silence, and she tapped her phone.

"Hi, Sarah," Mr. Pike said, smiling up out of the screen. "Just checking in. Everything okay there?"

"Yes, sir," Sarah said. "We're watching scary movies."

"Hi, Dad," Lori called out off-screen.

Mr. Pike smiled.

"Hi, honey," he said. "So, everything's under control?"

"Yes sir," Sarah said.

"Very good. Oh, and tell your friends not to get into my liquor cabinet."

Sarah paled. Mr. Pike nodded.

"It's okay," he said. "I don't mind a few friends. But I'm trusting you to be responsible and remember my daughter is there."

Sarah held the phone up

"Everybody hear that?"

The others responded as a chorus, "Yes, sir."

"Okay, then," Mr. Pike said. "I'll be home as soon as I can."

"Thank you, sir,"

Sarah hung up.

Danielle was staring darts at her, before tossing one last, lingering glare at Robbie, and turning about-face, stalked back outside.

Robbie frowned apologetically at Sarah, then followed Danielle out.

Kenny pointed to Deb's bottle of whiskey.

"You know," he said, "I think I'd like a drink."

Deb nodded, shaking her head at Sarah, even as she twisted the seal on the bottle.

Outside, the voices were already rising, Danielle's the loudest: "You BASTARD!"

Sarah shut her eyes. Normally, she wasn't much for alcohol, but a drink sounded pretty good to her right about now.

She turned to see Lori standing in the kitchen door, a solemn, serious expression on her face, as she held up the keys to her father's liquor cabinet.

Sarah half-smiled, taking the keys, as outside, the fireworks quickly began to escalate.

CHAPTER 10

Wyatt told Sarah six-thirty, and sure enough, promptly at the ass-crack of dawn, a boat-horn sounded out on her dock.

Sarah had already roused her house-guests. Deb fussed about the kitchen, making eggs and toast, as Sarah set-out the itinerary for the day.

Kenny frowned over his coffee.

"We're going out with *Wyatt*?"

"Don't worry," Sarah said. "You and Deb get your own boat."

Now, there was a knock on the back door. Grumbling, Sarah got up to answer. Her robe billowed, and Kenny's eyes flickered briefly after her exposed leg – earning a swat on the nose as Deb refilled his coffee.

"Morning, ma'am," Wyatt said formally, as Sarah let him in. "Running late?"

Sarah's lips pursed. She flapped her robe.

"A little. Give me five-minutes."

She disappeared into her room, changing quickly, dressing in layers, for a cold morning and sunny day on the lake. When she returned, Wyatt was standing over the kitchen table, going over her itinerary with Deb and Kenny.

Wyatt looked up as Sarah joined them.

"Well?" he asked. "You're our expert. What's the plan?"

"Here," Sarah said, pointing to a map of the lake with several areas high-lighted in red. "I compiled temperature-records from the last ten years and found a number of hot-spots. Probably areas where geothermal pressure has broken through the lake bed."

More than a dozen areas were circled over the length of the twenty-five-mile lake.

"Basically," Sarah said, "we go out to each of these spots, toss out a line and see what we can catch."

Kenny looked doubtful – Sarah had shown them the seven-pound razor-toothed fish she'd caught, kept on ice in the freezer.

"Hold on. You want us to catch a *piranha*?"

"Sure," Sarah said. "It's just a fish. Be careful of the teeth."

"And don't fall in the water," Wyatt added, "or they'll eat you alive."

Sarah frowned at Wyatt, but then turned back to Kenny.

"*Don't* fall in the water," she said.

She held up several lures, all prepared with a ten-inch length of wire, and gave them to Kenny.

"It's off-season," Wyatt said. "So *I* grant you special permission."

Kenny cast Wyatt a dire-eye.

"Thank you *so* much," he said.

Wyatt glanced at Sarah, expressionless, and winked.

Sarah actually snickered – Wyatt had an ornery-streak.

Kenny and Deb loaded up the old cruiser, Sarah's parents' old boat – heavier-bodied, more on the luxurious side, better-suited to the deeper, south-side route past Devil's Island.

"Text me what you find," Sarah instructed.

She and Wyatt would take the north. Wyatt grabbed-up Sarah's bags for her, again offering her a hand into the boat. Sarah rolled her eyes.

"Head towards Purgatory Cove," she said.

Wyatt nodded.

"But first," he said, as he steered them out into the cove, "I need to have a quick word with your neighbor."

Sarah felt a moment of panic as she realized Wyatt was steering them towards the Pike-house. The coward in her almost asked Wyatt to take her back.

Instead, she fell silent.

Wyatt glanced at her.

"You alright, ma'am?"

"I'm fine," she replied crisply.

Wyatt sidled-up to the Pike-property's boat-dock, tying off quickly, extending a helping hand to Sarah up the ladder.

It was now past seven. The man who answered when they knocked introduced himself as Dave, the supervisor, greeting them with raised brows when he saw Wyatt's badge.

"How can I help you, Officer Wyatt?" he asked, the very model of PR-spokesmen courtesy.

"Is the lady of the house available?" Wyatt asked.

"I can speak for her," Dave assured him.

This, Sarah thought, must be one of Lori's 'handlers'.

"Well," Wyatt began, "we had an incident yesterday..."

He was interrupted, however, by a voice behind Dave.

"Sarah...?"

Lori was standing in the hallway, hair-tossed, wearing the rumpled t-shirt and cut-offs she'd slept in.

The last time Sarah saw her, Lori was not-quite thirteen, going-on thirty, full of energy and boundless confidence.

Now, that light had darkened into neon, highlighted by semi-permanent circles under her eyes.

Dave and Wyatt both fell silent.

Finally, Sarah stepped forward, extending her arms. After an instant's hesitation, Lori accepted the awkward embrace.

"It's good to see you, Lori," Sarah said, pulling back, taking her hand. "It's been too long."

Lori's eyes cut away, shamefaced.

"I know," she said. "I'm sorry, I just sort of fell off the Earth. I... wasn't real proud of my situation."

Sarah smiled, giving her hands a squeeze.

"Believe me," she said, "I understand."

She glanced over at Wyatt and Dave.

"Listen. We can talk later. Any time you want. I'm just a phone-call away." She met her eye deliberately. "I always was."

Lori nodded.

"Not to interrupt your reunion, Miss Pike," Wyatt said, "but there are a couple of things we need to talk about."

Lori's eyes turned to Wyatt, and her posture abruptly changed.

Now Sarah saw the years in-between, as her former pre-tween babysitting-charge regarded Wyatt, who was tall and square-shouldered.

Sarah remembered twelve-year-old Lori's hyper-interest in boys, her crush on Robbie, but now she saw how the adult woman had learned to relate to men. Sarah could imagine her adapting the same pose to smooth-over a traffic-cop, arching her back, tossing her hair.

"What can I do for *you*, Officer Wyatt?" she asked.

Men, Sarah thought tiredly. Why did that bullshit *always* work on them?

Still, Wyatt remained all-business. He raised a mild eyebrow at the display, but kept his eyes deliberately on hers.

"I hate to tell you this, ma'am, but as of now, Lake Perdition is closed to the public."

Lori blinked, the flirtatious armor dropping.

"What are you talking about? This camp is supposed to open in two weeks."

Wyatt shook his head.

"Unfortunately, that might be dangerous. As of now, I'm putting an emergency halt on all water-activities on the lake until further notice."

"You can just *do* that?"

Wyatt shrugged.

"I'm doing it."

Dave, the supervisor, stepped-in quickly.

"Officer Wyatt," he objected, "this seems fairly extreme. What exactly is the danger?"

"Well," Wyatt replied, deliberately addressing Lori, "remember old Artie Langstrom? He was eaten alive by something in the lake yesterday morning, up on the rapids."

"*Eaten?*" Dave exclaimed. "Eaten by what?"

Wyatt glanced at Sarah.

"Tell them," he said.

Sarah eyed Lori levelly.

"He was killed by piranha," she said. "Specifically, *black* piranha. They're out on the lake in numbers. I caught a seven-pounder yesterday."

Lori glanced involuntarily back where the old koi ponds used to be.

"You think...?"

Sarah nodded.

"Wait a minute," Dave interrupted. "Piranha? In Idaho?"

He looked around at the apparently-serious faces staring back.

Then a quiet voice spoke up behind them.

"Excuse me?"

They turned to find Anne, Amy, and Donna standing in a trio behind them.

"Um," Anne ventured, "has anybody seen Dana, Adrienne, or Jack? They aren't in their rooms, and we can't find them anywhere."

"The last time I saw them," Donna said, "they were taking one of the boats out. They were going skiing." She looked worried. "That was yesterday."

Wyatt cast a grim eye in Sarah's direction.

"I think we better get out on the lake," he said.

Dave's supervisor-face suddenly etched with concern – a front-desk liability/responsibility reaction. He looked out the front window.

"One of the boats is gone," he said. He looked back at Wyatt. "Should I call for a search chopper?" he asked.

Wyatt shook his head.

"Not yet. I'll call myself if we need one. But an air-search in the morning is problematic because of the mist. But we've already got people out on the water." He nodded to Amy, Anne, and Donna. "We'll see if we can't find your friends, ladies."

Dave turned to Lori.

"I will call your father's lawyers," he told her, "and inform them of these developments."

Wyatt nodded to Sarah.

"Ma'am?" he said. "We'd better be on our way."

Sarah gave Lori's hand a last squeeze.

"You've got my number," she said.

Lori, still processing the news that her new-start/last-chance venture to change her life might be evaporating right before her eyes, nodded mutely.

Outside, the sun was not yet visible through the mist but the ambient light announced its presence, frosting the lake in a smoky haze.

Wyatt offered his helping hand to Sarah, as they clambered back aboard his boat. As he pushed off the dock into the cove, he shook his head sadly.

"Pretty girl, that Miss Pike," he said. "But for such a young gal, she looks ridden-hard and put-away-wet."

Sarah didn't answer, but couldn't argue.

Back at the house, Lori stood at the window, looking out, watching their boat disappear into the mist.

Then her eyes turned helplessly to where her father's koi ponds had once been, and groaned aloud at the picture forming in her mind.

CHAPTER 11

Dawn came slowly on the misty lake, but sound traveled fast and far.
South of Devil's Island, voices drifted, echoing – arguing.

Dana and Adrienne had just spent the night in the Boneyard, clinging
to a tree. Their boat drifted lazily just beneath them, sunk to the railing.

In the hours after Jack was killed, the two of them had fallen
variously to weeping, bickering, and calling for help.

Then it got dark.

To describe what it was like to be trapped out on Lake Eerie at night,
was a trauma all its own. Even crying out for rescue only brought a
responding cacophony of birds and animals – either that or evil
screaming spirits – who could tell?

"This was *your* idea," Dana reminded Adrienne. "All because you
were hot for some pretty-boy."

Adrienne glared back.

"Are you not bothered he was eaten alive?"

"Hell, *yeah*, I'm bothered," Dana replied, "but right now, I'm a little
more worried about *us*. He's already dead, and I barely knew him."

"So what do you want *me* to do about it? Swim for help?"

They stared at each other balefully, both of them wet and shivering.

Then there was a flash of light from out on the lake. Adrienne's head
perked.

"Did you see that?"

The light flashed again.

"That's a boat," Dana said. She peered into the fog. "*Hey!*" she
shouted. "*Help!*"

The light turned in their direction.

"Oh, thank God," Adrienne said, standing up on her branch.

Immediately, the both of them erupted in loud cries for help.

Now they heard a motor, and a spotlight framed them in their tree.
Voices carried across the water from behind the light.

"Jesus, Josh, it's a couple of girls!"

A boat materialized out of the mist, a fourteen-foot outboard, with
two men aboard, adorned with fishing gear. One of them was standing,
holding the light.

Adrienne and Dana waved and shouted. The man with the light
waved back.

"Easy, ladies, we're coming to get you." He glanced back. "Careful through these trees, Josh. It gets shallow."

Josh obliged, guiding them easily under Dana and Adrienne's tree. The man with the light shined it up into the branches.

"Morning, ladies," he said, "My name's Paul."

Paul extended a hand to Adrienne, who clambered down into the boat beside him. As Dana followed a moment later, he looked over at their sunken wreck.

"What happened? Did you ladies hit a tree?"

Dana and Adrienne exchanged glances. Adrienne pointed to the ragged mass, still floating by its life-jacket, less than twenty-yards away.

Paul frowned, nodding to Josh, who goosed the motor, turning them that way. Paul prodded the flotsam with a gaff-hook – the mass turned in the water.

A picture painted a thousand words.

Overnight, Jack's skeletonized corpse had gone white and fish-like, with a few clinging worms and water-beetles.

Dana turned and gagged.

"*Jesus*," Paul whistled through his teeth. "What did this?"

"He was water-skiing," Adrienne said. "He fell in. That's how he came out."

Josh's phone was beeping behind him.

"Hey, Paul," he said. "I'm getting an alert from the lake website."

He glanced up at Adrienne, and Dana, still gagging over the side.

"Looks like you ladies have been reported missing," he said, scrolling down. "And..."

Josh frowned, reading further. His eyes flicked out to the floating, cannibalized corpse

"It also looks like your friend here isn't the first."

He held up the screen to the others.

"*Piranha?*" Paul read doubtfully. "In *Idaho?*"

He looked at the flesh-stripped skeleton in the water.

"We better call Wyatt," he said.

Josh shook his head.

"He's gonna wonder why we're out here a day ahead of the season."

"We've got a dead guy," Paul said, pulling out his phone. "And a couple passengers to take care of," he said. "Maybe the SOB can cut us a break."

He swiped his screen awake and searched the number.

CHAPTER 12

Wyatt was carefully threading their way through Purgatory Cove when his phone rang in his pocket. He put it on speaker as he answered.

"This is Wyatt."

"Paul Mullins here, sir. Me and my brother just found those boaters you put out that bulletin for."

"What kind of condition are they in?"

"Well, sir," Paul replied, "the two girls are pretty cold and wet. But I'm afraid the fella... well, he didn't make it."

There was a pause on the line.

"I've never seen anything like it, Officer Wyatt. He's been eaten to the bones."

"Where are you?"

"Out in the Boneyard."

"Hang on."

Wyatt turned to Sarah. "Mitchell ought to be heading their way," he said. "Call and tell him to keep an eye out."

Sarah nodded, pulling out her own phone, touching Kenny's number.

"Put him on speaker," Wyatt instructed, returning to his own call.

"Listen up, Mullins. I've got people headed your way. You tell them everything they want to know, and then you take those two girls back to the Pike-house. Pamela is the on-site nurse. Have her check those young ladies out.

"Do that," Wyatt added, "and I might forget to ask what you were doing out on the lake, when opening day wasn't until tomorrow."

"We were just getting a good camping spot," Paul said.

"Well, I guess you didn't check the website," Wyatt said. "The lake is closed until further notice. I posted it yesterday."

"I've got them," Sarah said. "They're close."

She held up her phone to Wyatt.

"You hear me, Mitchell?"

"I'm here," Kenny answered.

"Your itinerary for the day has changed. We've got another dead body on the lake. I need you to transport the remains to the coroner's office in town."

"Wait a minute," Deb said in the background, "you mean, in our boat, with us?"

"Please inform the authorities," Wyatt continued, "interview and secure contact information for the witnesses. Miss Campbell and I will continue our investigation on the lake."

"Why can't you take the body back on your boat?" Kenny asked.

"Because Miss Campbell is the expert you brought in, and she's with me. You can come catch piranha tomorrow. Now, do you see them yet?"

After a moment's pause, Kenny affirmed.

"Yeah," he said. "I'm turning towards them now."

"Okay, Mullins," Wyatt said into his phone, "our people are on the scene. Cooperate, you and your brother can go sleep at home tonight. I'd throw you in jail just for being on the lake, but you might have saved those girls' lives, so I'll cut you slack."

Wyatt held up the phone, as if looking at Paul Mullins directly.

"*Once,*" he said.

"Yes, sir," Paul replied dolefully.

There was chatter in the background, from both Sarah and Wyatt's speakers as the two boats on the other side of the lake connected.

"Okay," Kenny said. "We've got them."

"Can you see the body?" Sarah asked.

There was more muttering in the background, before Kenny came on again.

"Yeah," he said. "Oh, *Jesus...*"

And somewhere behind him, Deb's voice, "Oh my *God...*"

"Well, Mullins," Wyatt said, "sounds like you're in good hands."

He clicked his phone off, and nodded to Sarah, who tapped Kenny off her speaker.

"Keep us posted," she said, and hung up.

"Well," Wyatt said grimly, "that's two dead in two days. Would you say this beats the Amazon average?"

"Not just attacks," Sarah replied, nodding, "but full-on frenzies. Your Mr. Mullins said 'eaten to the bone'."

There was only one explanation.

"They must be starving," she said.

"You said the population was healthy," Wyatt recalled.

"Yes. And their size indicates they were well-fed. At least until recently."

"Well," Wyatt said, considering, "at one time, there was a fish-hatchery that fed the lake"

"That's long gone."

"Then there was the catfish-invasion that convinced everyone to shut down the lake."

"Which also seems to be gone."

"Well," Wyatt said, "I'd say *that's* pretty self-explanatory."

Sarah also again noted the crystal-clarity of the water, absent of even normal clutter, no dropped leaves or branches – every last bit of organic debris.

Gobbled up.

"That leaves the most important question," Sarah said. "How are they breeding?"

She tapped her phone, bringing up her map, highlighting the hot-spots on the lake.

"Besides heat, they need underwater vegetation that can substitute for the long grasses in their native habitat. Any one of these areas located close to the bank, especially in coves, would be possible spots. My own lagoon has water lilies, and I found dead eggs gelled to the stems. It was too cold for them there, but those stalks were just what they were looking for."

Sarah tapped the screen again, bringing up the map of Devil's Island.

"Right here, we have two potentials. One is south of the island, right where our body was just found."

Now she pointed dead ahead.

"The other," she said, "is the falls."

CHAPTER 13

"Take us up to the shallows by the rapids first," Sarah instructed.

"Why?" Wyatt asked, eying the rocks.

"It's a wide patch, with a lot of lilies, just like in my lagoon."

Wyatt obliged, hovering cautiously along the green carpet of floating petals. Any further, visibility below the surface was zero.

"Get as close as you can," Sarah said, picking up a boat-hook. "I'm a little leery about sticking my arm down there. If there *are* eggs, the parents will guard them."

She reached the hook under the nearest plant-stalk, keeping her hands respectfully clear of the water.

"You won't usually get them feeding at breeding sites," she explained, "but they're hot spots for aggression. Incidents involving disturbed nests are usually individual bites from the parents. But if they happen to be clustered together in the same breeding site? Like, say, a congested population with limited suitable habitat? That accelerated aggression could very well make any of these nesting grounds extremely dangerous."

Sarah jerked the lily up by the root, its tendrils pulling away from the light layer of earthen muck that coated the otherwise hard lava lake-bed.

She held up the stalk.

Sure enough, there were eggs gelled all along its base. And just like in her own lagoon, they were discolored and dead.

Sarah looked around the cove. Yesterday, she caught a sixteen-inch fish on her fist cast. Today, they didn't seem in evidence.

Just to make sure, she took out her rod for a few experimental casts.

There were no bites.

Sarah frowned, trying to second-guess natural behavior of an animal in a foreign environment.

"They're hiding somewhere," she said, reeling in her line. "Or, if they really are shoaling together, they might be on the move."

"So, where now?" Wyatt asked.

"Let's head to the Boneyard," Sarah said. "We know they've been there too."

She tapped a quick text to tell Kenny they were headed their way.

"*Already on our way back to town,*" was Kenny's texted reply.

Then a moment later, from Deb, *"And I've got a cannibalized corpse bumping around under my feet."*

Sarah tapped a pain-faced icon back. *"Sorry."*

Wyatt steered them back into deeper water, as they toured-around the southern point of Devil's Island, before turning back towards the Boneyard, transitioning from hazardous shallow rocks, to an obstacle-course of trees and loose-floating logs.

Sarah kept her eye peeled along the bank, looking for patches of vegetation, particularly outcroppings of lilies. Twice, she spotted likely areas, and Wyatt stopped, but repeated casts brought up nothing.

Then, just ahead of the Boneyard, they came across the same floating mass Jack had spotted the day before.

Overnight, the moose-carcass had drifted. Wyatt pulled the boat up alongside, and Sarah latched-on with a gaff.

"Did the damned fish kill this animal?" Wyatt asked.

Sarah looked down at the skeletonized corpse, that was probably twelve-hundred pounds in life. That was the thing about piranha – they didn't leave enough behind to tell if a bite was postmortem or not.

"Well," she said, running her hand over a circular-divot that could have fit a pool-ball, "this moose could have simply died, and if it wound-up in the water, they would certainly go right after it.

"But," she allowed, "there *was* a case in Brazil, where a full-grown workhorse got attacked after farmhands tried to lead it across a narrow river-channel. By the time they were able to pull the horse on shore, its guts were already hollowed-out and the fish were flooding out of its empty torso."

"I always heard they could eat a cow in a minute," Wyatt said. "Well, they sure did a number on this guy. You think it was sixty-seconds or less?"

Sarah ran her fingers along a series of golf-ball-sized bites that sheared away bone.

"I'll bet it was close," she said.

She unhooked the gaff, letting the moose fall back into the water.

As she did so, her jacket caught on the cusp of its horn, and pulled her right towards the water with it.

Sarah jerked back with a start, catching the railing, stepping back to find Wyatt already latched onto her arm.

"Careful, Miss," he cautioned.

Her heart hammering, Sarah shook his hand loose.

"I'm fine," she said, curtly.

She glanced around the grove of sunken trees.

Were the fish even there? They were gone from the rapids.

What, Sarah wondered, might be different?

They were still in relatively deep water, so before they ventured into the Boneyard among the trees, Sarah tossed out one more cast.

This time, something hit her line right away.

"Whoa," Sarah said, as the rod bent in her hands. "This is *big*."

A *lot* bigger than the seven-pound fish she caught yesterday.

Whatever was on the line began to fight. Wyatt raised an eyebrow at the jerking rod.

"You got that okay, Miss?" he asked.

Sarah cast him an irritated eye.

"I've got it," she assured him.

Then there was a flurry of activity, nearly jerking the pole out her hands. Forty-yards out, a nearly five-foot catfish broke the surface, struggling with the line in its mouth.

The water frothed around it, as squat, fat black shapes battened down, mobbing, frenzied.

Wyatt let out a slow whistle.

The battling catfish disappeared below the surface, and for several moments the furor underwater continued.

Then it all went still and the line went heavy and dead.

Sarah reeled it in, knowing exactly what she would find.

She dragged the devoured carcass up to the side of the boat.

"One of those invasive catfish," Wyatt remarked. "Still a few hanging around, I guess. One less, now. He's a biggin'"

Sarah nodded.

"A giant *Wels* catfish," she identified. "A native of eastern Europe. This was also one of Leo Pike's pond-fish, a more obvious, and initially-successful invader. Although things have clearly changed."

Sarah looked down its gullet, out the hole that had replaced its throat. The mouth was nearly ten-inches across.

"At this size," Sarah said, "this fish would have been a rival, if not a direct predator of piranha. But the second it started to struggle on the line, it instantly became a target." She looked down at the bits of hide still clinging to the spine.

"And that's the key word," she said. "*Instantly*."

She dropped the catfish-head onboard and pointed ahead to the Boneyard.

"Okay," she said. "Let's take a look."

Wyatt led them slowly into the hooded grove of half-submerged trees.

"Wait," Sarah said, holding up a hand. "Do you hear a *popping* sound?"

Wyatt shut down the motor and they drifted to a stop.

After a moment, there was a loud *burp*.

"There," Sarah said. "You heard that?"

A puff of steam belched-up through the water surface, followed by a steady stream of bubbles from below.

"That's a vent," Sarah said. She pointed to the nearest tree. "Here, take us over there."

Wyatt turned the motor back on, following directions, drifting smoothly beside the half-submerged trunk of a large hemlock tree.

Sarah reached her gaff down, feeling for the spot where the silt on the lake-bed started to erode around the roots.

She kept an eye on the surrounding water – so eerily clear. She knew the fish must be there, somewhere, but she still hadn't spotted one.

Piranha could seem skittish, and they tended to stay out of sight. But that was true of all ambush predators.

Keeping her hands clear of the water, she dug the hook along the tree root. When she pulled it up, there was clear jelly and eggs clinging to the end.

Sarah nodded grimly to Wyatt. These were fresh. Viable. She scraped samples into a jar, and reached down again with the gaff.

As she did so, a black shape rocketed out of nowhere and struck the metal hook, nearly yanking it out of her hand.

Sarah started backwards, reaching for the railing.

This time, however, she missed.

In a complete forward, rolling somersault, Sarah fell forward out of the boat into the lake.

Her first sensation was, yes, the water *was* warmer here – she could tell the difference right away, as if an underwater funnel was pumping right into the lake.

The first visual observation was flashing black shapes, scattering at first, but then turning and coming for her from all directions.

In the clear water, she saw the teeth.

Something hit her leg, then her arm, and her hip, before she was grabbed by the scruff of the neck and yanked roughly clear of the water.

In the half-instant it all happened, Sarah flashed-back to childhood, and being snatched out of their neighbor's wading pool by her mother – she had been misbehaving, not coming when she was called.

Sarah blinked, dripping and sputtering, as Wyatt set her on her feet, like a pet cat.

She looked back at the water, which was still churning, then down at her legs, and realized she was bleeding.

"Oh my God," she said. "I'm *bit*."

There were three sizable holes chopped right out of her jeans and jacket. Sarah started poking gingerly at her hip when Wyatt abruptly grabbed her, bent her over his knee, popped out a pocket-knife and slit her pants at the hip.

Sarah chirped in outrage, before she saw the blood seeping from the cup-shaped divot bitten out of her.

"Sorry, ma'am," Wyatt said professionally, as he split her pant-leg the rest of the way down her leg to the other bite – still nasty, but not nearly as deep. He had already grabbed an old rusted first-aid box, and Sarah suppressed a shriek as he poured rubbing alcohol over both wounds. Then there was the stretch of tape as he patched gauze and a bandage over her hip.

Sarah submitted to the indignity docilely enough as she realized how close it had just been.

"I think your denim saved you from the worst of it," Wyatt said. He moved methodically from her hip to her leg wound, bending her like a doll.

"Whatever got your leg, mostly got a mouthful of Levi's," he said, "but the one on your hip's pretty bad." He applied a last strap of tape. "I'd say stitches, but there's nothing to stitch. It's just patching a hole. Not *too* deep. But I'd keep an eye on it."

He gave a cursory check on her arm, which was only slightly cut – the cup-shaped hole in her jacket was the worst of that one.

Now Sarah stood there, sans-pants. She had actually dressed in layers, with swimwear underneath, and was already thinking of stripping-down in the midday-heat. But now, even with the sun, her exposed skin shivered in gooseflesh.

She hadn't even felt the bites, beyond the sheer impact. Somehow, that was worse – the thought of just being utterly devoured, in moments, before the pain even had a chance to reach your brain – still active and aware for those last few moments – long enough to look down and *see...*

Sarah realized Wyatt had just saved her life. He had pulled her clear a bare-instant before she would have been hit with the full weight of the mob. It would have taken seconds.

Wyatt eyed her neutrally.

"Are you going to be alright, ma'am? You need a doctor?"

Sarah tapped the bandage on her hip, gingerly. She sighed. Wyatt was right. There was nothing to stitch. First-aid was already rendered.

"No," she said. "But I think I'm ready to call it a day." She held up her jar of fish-eggs. "I got at least some of what I was after.

"And," she said, resigned, "I think you got your answer regarding potential danger."

CHAPTER 14

Lori hadn't been to the hot-springs in years.

It had been one of her favorite spots as a kid – much to her father's disapproval. The springs were unstable and sometimes dangerous. You could get excessive thermal-heat. You might also discover bears liked to take a soak once in a while, although that wasn't much of a problem anymore, with no fish to attract them to the lake in the first place.

Lori smiled, remembering her father actually installed a Jacuzzi-tub at the house just to keep his willful daughter at home.

Of course, just when she could use it, that hot-tub was the one thing the construction-crew hadn't repaired – something about the twelve-year-old model-tub using too much power.

Lori had spent most of the morning in her room, while they all waited on word of their missing councilors.

Her lawyers, however, had already called.

According to Dave, the short answer was, *yes*, the camp not-opening meant she would fail to meet the terms of her probation.

Dave placed a sympathetic hand on her shoulder. Lori resisted the urge to pull away.

"That doesn't mean they're going to cart you off to jail. It's reasonable that other arrangements can be made. These are not circumstances within your control."

Lori nodded agreeably. It seemed nothing was going to be in the foreseeable future.

"On the other hand," Dave added reluctantly, "there *is* the matter of money. This property is your last asset. The camp was an investment that might now be a total loss."

That was not to mention the unresolved missing-persons situation, but Dave wasn't bringing that up yet. Brass-tacks were first.

"The lawyers that fix this stuff for you need to be paid," he said. "And if they aren't, they stop fixing."

Lori absorbed this silently. She was not surprised, but had still promptly retreated back to her room. She didn't want to be seen worrying about herself.

The rest of the house gathered in the kitchen, where Henry prepared breakfast. Amy and Anne sat at the table, looking worried and somber.

When Lori didn't show, Pamela came knocking on her door with a plate of eggs, hotcakes and toast.

"Here, honey," she said. "Henry made this for you."

Lori smiled, taking the plate.

Pamela shook her head.

"You know, Henry and I noticed those kids had gone off," she said. "But we just figured they all ended-up stirring the Kool-Aid back in their rooms. I wish we would have said something."

Lori got the official word not long after that. Dave came to her room and told her what happened to Jack Burrell.

"I've already notified your lawyers," he said. "It's early on, and the situation is fluid, but there shouldn't be any direct liability. Unfortunately, if the authorities trace the first source from your father's fish ponds back to this property, which you still own, that creates a potential risk, if a bereaved family member tries to sue."

The fishermen's boat arrived with Adrienne and Dana a short while later.

Dave met them at the dock, accepting tearful hugs from both girls, and shaking the hands of the two burly young fishermen, who introduced themselves as Josh and Paul.

Amy and Anne also ran out, joining the group-hug, even though they had all known each other less than a day.

Lori watched from her back porch. Once upon a time, no matter what the ruckus, she would have been climbing over the fence just to be a part of it.

Now? On her own dock? She hung-back. And she wished everyone would just go away. This house, for all its haunted past, was all she had left.

"Kinda sucks, doesn't it?" Henry said, sidling-up beside her, in his apron. "When it was once *your* place?"

Henry frowned, a cheated burn on his brow.

"This lake was home to a lot of us," he said. "Your daddy's hatchery was our livelihood. Hell, it was the life-blood of the lake."

He patted a hand on her shoulder, a gesture Lori accepted from Henry without thought.

"A lot's been taken from all of us, girl," he said.

"Ain't that the truth, honey," Pamela said, passing them as she came out of the house with her nurse's kit.

The volume of chatter, rising on the dock as everyone tried to tell their story at once, ceased as Pamela cut loose a piercing, silencing whistle, tapping her nursing hat, and motioning Dana and Adrienne to her heel. Josh and Paul stepped aside, as both girls complied meekly.

Watching from the kitchen, Henry looked sadly after his wife.

"Look at her," Henry said, as Pamela gave Adrienne and Dana a strict once-over. "She's still compensating."

He shook his head.

"You lose things. You lost your father when you were young. Pamela and I lost our son when *he* was young. No reason for it. Leukemia. And because our damn doctor told us we might have stopped it if they'd caught it sooner, Pamela thinks because she's a nurse, she should have caught it herself."

Lori knew Henry and Pamela had lost a son – their 'damn doctor' had been Danielle's father, Dr. Taylor.

Henry smiled sadly.

"Funny. I'm the one that still likes to talk about him. She never talks about him at all. It was harder on her. Not just because she was his mother, but because he took after her. He looked like her. Acted like her."

"What was his name?" Lori asked.

"His name was Jason." Henry nodded to Pamela, bent at Adrienne and Dana's knee. "And look at her. Still out saving everybody else. Never saying his name."

Dave, meanwhile, was grilling Josh and Paul. Lori figured he would be reporting their story back to her father's lawyers.

"Have you spoken with authorities?" Dave asked the two fishermen.

"Just Wyatt," Josh said. "He told us to take the girls home. He said someone might be asking us questions in the next few days."

"He also told us the lake's closed," Paul reminded him. "If we can't camp, we've gotta get moving."

Dave glanced back at the house. "We're set up for guests," he said. "You're welcome to stay here, tonight. It's the least I can offer."

Lori glanced at Henry, who shrugged helplessly, shaking his head, as he turned back to his kitchen.

Yeah, sure, Lori thought, eyeing Dave narrowly, just invite whoever you want to sleep at this house that isn't yours. It's the least you can do.

Dana and Adrienne, on the other hand, greeted the idea enthusiastically, with Pamela actually holding Adrienne down in her chair as she doctored her up.

"Easy, honey," the older woman chided. "No need to throw it *that* hard." She glanced back at Josh and Paul. "Those two dogs'll come sniffing, just like they always do."

Amy and Anne weren't subtle either, Lori thought.

"Oh, you should definitely stay," Amy said, latching onto Josh's arm, even as Anne hooked onto Paul. Pamela pushed Adrienne back down again as she stood to interject.

Josh and Paul traded grins.

"I guess we can stay," Paul allowed. Josh nodded agreement.

Dave smiled at the girls, rolling his eyes.

"Okay, fellas," he said, turning to the two fishermen. "Let me find you a room."

He turned, and as they approached the house, Lori quickly faded back inside, retreating to her room, not answering the brief knock when Dave led Josh and Paul down to what had once been her father's office. The sound of college-girl giggles followed from outside.

Twenty-minutes later, Lori had ducked out of the house. She'd either been headed to the Cauldron or to the hot-springs.

If she'd gone to the Cauldron, her intention would have been to jump-off.

Here at the springs, she was thinking drowning. After all, people had fallen into the Cauldron's pit before and just broken a leg.

The sun was angling into afternoon, and the bubbling ponds were like blinding mirrors.

Lori looked around the grounds and saw litter. She shook her head sadly. People used to self-police at the springs – they respected the natural resource.

For some reason, that bit of litter depressed her more than all the rest, like the last drop on the candle.

God, she just didn't want to wake up and see the next day anymore.

Just wade out there, she thought. Find a deep part of the pond, let herself sink down to the bottom, and take a deep breath. Then it would all be done.

Lori kicked a half-eaten bag of Cheetos into the water.

She shut her eyes.

But instead of marching forward into the waiting springs, she turned, and headed back down the trail for home.

She would wait and see what happened tomorrow.

No sense jumping until you knew all the reasons why.

She looked down at her phone, where Sarah had left her number, and she nearly tapped the screen.

Instead, she shut it off and stuck it back in her pocket.

Behind her, the bubbling hot-springs bustled the floating bag of Cheetos Lori had kicked into the water.

Then something snapped it up from below.

74

CHAPTER 15

When Wyatt turned them back into Sarah's cove, it was late afternoon and her little lagoon was already covered in the shadows of the surrounding hills.

By now, her butt was throbbing.

She couldn't even fairly be said to have been bitten on the ass – more that little slope on her hip, above her left butt-cheek. Not quite a tramp-stamp.

But her whole left glute felt like a balloon.

Wyatt noticed her wince as, this time, she was more accepting of help out of the boat. When she bent to gather her bags, he simply gathered them up and carried them into the house.

It was still daylight, but the house was dark, and Sarah switched-on the lights. She'd been back one night, with Deb and Kenny both over, but that wasn't yet enough to chase that stale, empty smell away.

She also hadn't spent the night alone. She glanced out the window, at the fading daylight.

Wyatt set Sarah's bags down, tipping his hat as he prepared to leave.

"Wait," she said. "Sit down a minute. You probably saved my life today. That's worth at least coffee and a biscuit."

Wyatt glanced at his watch, but nodded agreeably.

Sarah retreated briefly to her bedroom, doffing her wet clothes, and donning baggy sweats – nice and loose over her throbbing glute.

When she returned, she found him perusing her family pictures on the wall. Sarah would have been sixteen in the most recent images, reflecting concurrent hair-styles, always the most casual in Sarah's case.

But the biggest difference was a bright and unaffected sixteen-year-old smile. That was gone for good.

Wyatt turned as she came in.

"Nice looking family," he said.

Sarah nodded, turning on the water, putting coffee in the grinder, grabbing a biscuit for the toaster oven.

"Yeah," she said. "I miss them."

"I'd heard they'd passed," Wyatt said. "My condolences. Apologies if it's a sore spot."

Sarah shook her head.

"It's been a couple years."

Although, even as she said it, she looked at the bag of coffee in her hand – her mother's brand, as was the sugar, the creamer, and the expensive, fancier-than-it-needed-to-be coffee-maker itself – a snapshot into a life that was.

Sarah quickly wiped her eye, lest she appear to be tearing-up.

She looked at her reflection staring back from the window above the sink. When she was a kid, she always fancied the transparent images in glass were ghosts. She was also reminded how people always told her how much she favored her mother, a likeness that grew more pronounced as she'd grown older.

The ghost in the window was rather like the ghost of her mother looking back – except that it was *her*.

A ding sounded as the coffee-brewer finished. Sarah pulled two cups out of the cupboard, and filled them both up. She offered creamer to Wyatt, who shook his head.

"Black, please."

Not surprised, Sarah mused, doctoring her own judiciously.

As she turned, cups in hand, she thumped her hip on the counter, uttering a quick yelp as the tape on her bandage pulled loose.

"Still smarting, is it?" Wyatt asked. "You better let me take a look at that."

Sarah, still with hot-coffee in each hand, had not *quite* given consent when she was grabbed and bent over the kitchen table in the manner of plopping a mostly-cooperative dog into a bath – although she had to admit, Wyatt's rough, calloused hands were remarkably delicate, as he pulled back the elastic of her sweat-bottoms, and peeled the tape away, to inspect the wound.

"Ummm," Sarah said awkwardly. "How's it look?"

"Well," Wyatt said, "you basically got a hole here the size of a quarter. It got down past the skin into the fat, which means it's superficial, but it's going to leave a scar."

He pulled the dressing clear. It came away bloody.

"Have you got a first-aid kit?"

Sarah, still holding both cups and propped awkwardly over the table with her pants partially down, nodded towards the restroom. As Wyatt went to fetch more bandages, she took the opportunity to set down the coffee and inspect the bite herself.

She'd gotten it bleeding again, but it was amazing how clean the wound was – it was a perfect walnut-sized cup taken right out of her flesh.

That was after biting through her denim jeans, it sank that deep. And three of them hit her in less than a second. If Wyatt hadn't pulled her out...

"Here," Wyatt said, returning with bandages and alcohol, and unceremoniously folded her back over the table. She chirped at the fire-sting, as he dabbed her wound with alcohol.

"Sorry," he said, setting the old bloody rags aside.

There was the rip of tape as he applied a fresh bandage across the top of her buttocks with the efficiency of a UPS package.

"Okay," he said, stepping back to admire his work. "All done."

Sarah paused, poised over the table, tapping gingerly at her swollen and partially-exposed rump.

It was this pose Kenny and Deb trundled in on – made worse as Sarah, suddenly self-conscious, hopped to her feet, quickly hiking up her sweat-bottoms.

Wyatt looked up mildly.

"Just administering first-aid to the lady."

Kenny and Deb exchanged glances.

"Miss Campbell got bit," Wyatt said.

Sarah dipped her waistband over her bandage, as Wyatt explained briefly.

"Oh, *honey*," Deb said, taking Sarah's arm, fussing maternally. "Are you okay?"

"A couple bites," Sarah said, nodding. "It could have been a lot worse."

"Jesus," Kenny said, as Sarah pulled back the bandage over the more modest wound on her shoulder. "You were lucky."

Sarah indicated Wyatt.

"I was lucky *he* was there," she said.

"Wow," Deb said, looking at Wyatt with new respect. "You saved her life."

Kenny shook his head reproachfully at Sarah.

"If any one of us was going to fall in, it would be you. I remember when you fell into the Cauldron reservoir back in high school. You were lucky then, too, that Deb and *I* were there."

Kenny pulled out his phone, attaching it to the monitor on Sarah's desk.

"*Okay*," he said. "Here's what *we* did today."

"*This*," Deb added crossly, "was the part in the morgue *after* we dragged a piranha-eaten corpse for twenty-miles into town."

Kenny tapped the mouse, bringing up the coroner's snapshots of the body.

"Here's the initial medical report," he said, opening the file. "Almost exactly the same condition as Artie Langstrom, with a little bit of overnight exposure."

He brought up close-ups of the gruesome remains. There were spots, particularly the face, where entire chunks of bone were bitten away. Pool-ball-sized chunks.

Roosevelt's cow was supposedly taken in sixty-seconds by red-bellies, averaging one to two-pounds. The fish in this lake were the largest Sarah had ever seen.

"The idea," she said, "that a piranha-population could exist here at all, let alone be this robust, should be impossible."

"Well," Deb said, "what do we know? I think we have to assume the entry point must have been the Pike-farm."

Kenny nodded.

"After..." he cleared his throat. "After the accident, the property was empty and the power was off for a period of weeks. During that time, the ponds were solar-heated, but their pumps and irrigation were shut-down, so when it rained, they flooded."

"That," Deb said, "was indicated in the reports as the probable cause of the catfish invasion."

Wyatt leaned over the screen.

"Evidently piranha, too," he said. "But piranha have been introduced to North American lakes and rivers before. Just never successfully. What's different here?"

"Well," Sarah said, "for starters, these particular fish would have had a leg-up. They were farmed by Leo Pike. Their gene-pool would have been bred in ideal conditions, with the perfect temperature, low-stress, plenty of food. They would have been free of bacteria, infection. Strong, healthy, natural. And as acclimated as he could make them over repeated generations."

"So their survivability would have been high," Deb agreed. "And the area is practically busting with geothermal pressure. The lake floor is brittle and hollow, so it's quite possible the same source that created the hot-springs could also be producing isolated pockets of warm water. In shallow enough water, ideally a cove, that could allow for breeding."

"I found one today," Sarah said. "But with the numbers we're seeing, especially, at the size of these fish? Right up near the normal maximums for the species. There has to be other, larger nests. The Boneyard is hardly ideal. Any one of those coves where their eggs died would have been much better, but the thermal-heat is the deciding-factor."

"So," Kenny said, "assume you've got the environmental requirements for reproduction covered. Add a generationally-bred tolerance to cold. An introduced-species, absent of natural predators."

"*And*," Sarah added, "for at least a few important early years, they were still being fed by the hatchery."

Kenny nodded.

"But not anymore," Sarah said. "Now, in the closed environment of the lake, they have eaten every available bit of biomass they could find. No trout, barely any catfish. I found a dead moose today that might have been a carcass fallen in the lake, but it also might well have been eaten alive. Either way, it was a bare skeleton. That's the third direct evidence of swarming behavior on a human-sized or larger animal I've found within two days."

Sarah shook her head.

"They're attacking their own on the line. Becoming cannibals. They only do that in worst-case scenarios.

"I think," she finished grimly, "we are at a very dangerous point."

"After two deaths, I'd have to agree." Wyatt sighed. "I'm starting to think those missing college kids didn't get lost in the woods.

"So," he said, "now that these fish *are* here, and apparently breeding, what is the possibility they might get into some of the major rivers like the Snake or the Deschutes?"

"They wouldn't be able to breed in either of those rivers," Sarah assured him.

"They did here," Wyatt returned.

"We have unique conditions," Sarah replied.

"Which means they found a way," Wyatt said.

Sarah's lips pursed. Rather than argue circular logic, she simply conceded.

"I don't think," she said, "piranha could populate the surrounding rivers and waterways like they have here, but it would still be best not to give them the opportunity."

That seemed to satisfy him.

"Prognosis?" he asked.

"I can't even say until we've established the true extent of the problem." She shook her head. "For the moment, and immediate future, we have an unknown, unprecedented, and likely dangerous situation. Likely *very* dangerous."

"So what do we do about it?"

"Well," Sarah said, "first you go after their nests, so we need to find them. We've already got one, and two others where they've tried, one right here in my own cove. So we know what they're looking for. What they need is the heat. They aren't laying viable eggs in snow-melt, no matter how acclimated they are. They're not evolved for it."

"Okay," Wyatt said. "We find the nest. Then what? Pull it up? Poison it?"

Sarah looked over to Deb and Kenny. Kenny shrugged. Deb frowned.

"I'm an adviser here," Sarah said. "I would say we have to eliminate the nest somehow. But releasing poison, especially if it's widespread, is... problematic."

Wyatt turned a measured eye to Kenny.

"I'm guessing," he said, "most of those problems are regulatory red-tape. Wouldn't it be great if we had someone at the office."

Kenny deliberately met Wyatt's eye.

"I agree we need to destroy the nests," he said. "I'm not against recommending poisons, but I hope we can avoid it. It might be easier to just pull the nests out."

"You mean while the pissed-off parents are trying to bite your hands off?"

Wyatt let out a patient sigh.

"Look," he said, "I'm sorry, but I need a little more short-term advice on what to do right *now*."

"At this point," Sarah said, "my recommendation is simply stay clear of the water. That's not likely to change soon."

Wyatt nodded.

"So the lake stays closed," he said tiredly. "And now I gotta spend the next forty-eight hours chasing angry fishermen, telling them they have to leave because the fish *are* biting."

He shook his head.

"Mind if I toss something crazy at you?" he asked. "How about just authorizing a 'piranha-season'? Just let all those fishermen loose. No limits. Then we have a fish-fry. Eat 'em right back."

Kenny and Deb exchanged looks with Sarah who shrugged.

"Practically," she said, "that might actually work. Pit the predators against each other. And the natural enemy of fish is fishermen."

"Unfortunately," Kenny said, "there would be legal problems if someone else got hurt."

Wyatt shrugged.

"Just a thought. Sometimes us simple folk try to do things the easy way."

Wyatt stepped back from the table.

"Okay," he said. "All you smart folks seem to have your study guides set." He nodded to Sarah. "You are on your own tomorrow. It was supposed to be opening day and people are already on the road. I posted the closure online and told the radio-stations, but a lot won't hear it. And a lot of people just show-up anyway whether they heard it or not."

He regarded the three of them.

"If you see anyone on the lake, wave them down and tell them the area is closed to the public. Show them the notice on the site if they complain."

"Wait a minute," Kenny said. "I'm not a cop. This isn't our job."

"Well," Wyatt said, "yesterday, I gave you permission to fish. Today, I'm deputizing you. You're just getting all kinds of privileges."

"What if someone gives us trouble?"

"Mention my name," Wyatt said levelly.

Kenny glanced at Deb and Sarah, who both shrugged.

"You could also try telling them the water's full of carnivorous fish and show them those autopsy pictures on your phone. I'd post it on the website, except for respect to the families."

It would be a better deterrent than a no-trespassing sign, Sarah would admit.

"Which reminds me," Wyatt said, pulling his phone and tapping Norman's number. He waited patiently through nine rings until Norm picked up.

"Hello?" Norm answered. "Water-taxi reservations."

Wyatt gritted his teeth.

"Goddamn it, Norman," he said. "This is Wyatt. What the hell are you doing taking reservations?"

"I got two parties going out tomorrow," Norman replied.

"Oh, for..." Wyatt cursed silently. "Norman, you knew the season was on hold. Why'd you book charters?"

"They booked weeks ago. Just because the season's off, doesn't mean you can't go out on the lake."

"Well, yes, actually, right now, it does. Didn't you check the website?" But Wyatt sighed. "Never mind. Stupid of me to ask. Forget it. As of now, the lake is closed to the public. I'm going to need you out on the boat tomorrow, helping me patrol the lake."

"I already gave the keys to Robbie. He's out on his own tomorrow."

"Oh, perfect. Give me his number."

Norman read it off.

"Okay," Wyatt said. "Nobody else goes out on the lake. No charters. You see anybody else heading this way you tell them. Got it?"

Norman sounded a bit sullen.

"Got it."

Wyatt hung up, turning to the others.

"Well, folks," he said. "Be careful out there. We've got two dead people already. We don't need more."

He tipped his hat, as he stepped aside and let himself out the door.

"Miss him already," Kenny muttered. Deb swatted him but did not disagree.

Sarah, however, paused thoughtfully, watching out the window.

"What?" Kenny asked.

"I'll be right back," Sarah said, and followed Wyatt out the door.

CHAPTER 16

Wyatt was untying his boat. As Sarah walked up, he offered his typical, unsmiling greeting.

"Forget something, ma'am?"

"No," Sarah said. "I... well, I just wanted to tell you again, I appreciate what you did today."

Wyatt shrugged, stepping down into his boat.

"I hope anyone standing there would have done the same thing."

Sarah shook her head – not many who could have snatched her hundred and thirty pounds like a pet cat. If she'd been with Kenny and Deb, it would have been over.

"Are you planning to sleep on your boat?" Sarah asked. "I have an extra room."

Wyatt's lip curled-up at one corner – on another man, it might have been a smile.

"You askin' me to sleep over, ma'am?" He shook his head. "Actually, I have a place in town. I commute to the lake, but it's not my only territory. Other rivers and lakes need attention too."

He tapped the railing.

"But I've slept on the boat before," he said. "It's not a hardship for me. I like it out here. What could be better than sleeping out under the stars any time I want? It's why I do this."

Wyatt shrugged.

"I prefer it to living around a lot of people. Other folks seem to prefer it that way too."

Sarah nodded. She could see mutual advantage there.

She'd pegged him a control freak, but that wasn't it, after all.

It was about *escaping* control – tossing the shackles of the modern world.

Sarah actually could see the appeal. Even a certain nobility.

As he stood, stoic in the dimming light, she remembered he responded without even a blush to Lori's flirting, not awkward or embarrassed, or self-conscious.

Sarah wondered what noble would even look like, these days.

By all accounts, Wyatt was reputed to be one of the hardest-asses going, and Sarah had seen nothing on short-acquaintance to refute that.

But she would be lying if she didn't admit that ruggedness perversely appealed to her.

She understood her own psychology well enough to recognize it was the same way Robbie's juvie-badness once turned her on – although to be fair, it was probably a positive distinction.

The difference was she actually felt *safe* in Wyatt's company. People who had never felt afraid, might not appreciate that.

"So you're headed home?" Sarah asked.

"Not quite yet," Wyatt said. "I'm gonna spend a couple hours patrolling. Anybody camping will have a fire going, and that's easy to spot at night."

"Also," he said, pointing across the cove, "I wanna take a look-see over at your neighbor's place. Just to make sure they've got everything locked-down tonight."

Sarah looked across the water to the Pike-house. The lights were already misty and indistinct.

There was no music tonight.

Word was, the young man who'd been killed was a councilor that just arrived yesterday. Sarah wondered what liability Lori might have to bear.

Lori still hadn't called or texted. Sarah hadn't expected her to. At this point, she wasn't sure she even wanted her to.

Still, Sarah promised herself she would answer if that call came. She owed Lori that much.

She glanced back at her own house, where Kenny and Deb waited. Then she turned to Wyatt.

"If you're just going to tour the cove," she said, "I'd like to tag along. I need to see the night conditions on the lake."

Wyatt shrugged, offering up his hand. Favoring her wounded rump, she climbed down into the boat beside him. He pulled in the mooring rope, pushed off, and started the motor, turning out into the lagoon.

Sarah shivered a little in the wind. Once the sun released its hold on the mountain air, the chill quickly bit down. Wyatt kept a low speed, staying in deeper water, lest some underwater rock or log punch out their bottom. His eyes were steady, straight ahead.

Drifting down from the hillside, were the first echoes of the birds and wildcats as they began their nightly clamor of bloodcurdling howls, cries, and wailing to beat the damned.

Wyatt cast a brief glance over his shoulder.

"It can get a little spooky out here at night."

Sarah nodded, wiping gooseflesh from her arms.

"The truth is," she remarked, "it's probably *safer* right now. Piranha are sight-hunters that are inactive at night."

"You don't think we could wake them up?"

"I'm not saying we should try it," Sarah replied, "but there was a ferry that sank one night in the Amazon, right by the local dock, and all hundred-and-eight passengers were eaten alive by the night-fish in the river. Big piraiba and red-tailed catfish, piracatingas, but no piranha. And they were there. We know because they showed up in the morning to clean up what was left."

But Sarah held up a cautionary finger.

"That's not to say," she amended, "what holds true in their native habitat holds true here. The ferry-incident just shows how many dangerous fish live in the Amazon. Predators who coexist learn not to step on each other's toes. It might not be the case where they've lived in an absence of competitors."

"So, no midnight skinny-dippin'," Wyatt allowed.

Sarah blinked at the choice of words, wondering if it was intended to be suggestive, but his dour face never changed.

She turned her attention to the Pike-house, just ahead, perusing the renovations.

Most obvious was the dormitory-style housing where the koi ponds used to be, probably because Mr. Pike had already leveled the ground, and set the foundations for plumbing.

The nearest of the new buildings was right over the spot where the *S. rhombeus* pond had been.

Wyatt trolled the shoreline from a hundred yards out, looking for signs of activity. The lights were on in the house, and there was the flash-blink of a TV playing. Henry was in the kitchen, cleaning-up after dinner.

A shadow appeared at the living room window as Pamela peered out. Sarah wondered if she'd spotted their boat-lights.

"Ol' Pamela," Wyatt said. "She still sorta holds a grudge. I busted ol' Henry taking a deer off-season a few years back, and he ended-up doing a little time because it violated his probation."

Wyatt shrugged.

"What can I say? I'm sorry he did it. Jail sucks."

Sarah caught the inference.

"Been there?" she asked.

"A couple overnights," he acknowledged. "Drunk and disorderly. Bar-fights back in the Corps. I was eighteen. Got in more trouble with my commander for the fake ID."

Sarah nodded. She had never technically been in jail, although she *was* in the building for nearly twelve hours and not free to leave. She had just been sitting in a chair at a desk in a room by herself, rather than a different room designated as a 'holding-cell'.

Neither had she been arrested. All that time, was about asking questions.

"You were seventeen," Wyatt said, "the night of the accident."

Sarah nodded.

"We were kids," she said.

"Misbehaving teenagers," Wyatt said. "And somebody died. Not the first time."

Sarah's brow furrowed.

"Don't mean to offend," Wyatt added quickly. "It's a shame, is all. And I can see you're still wearing it. Twelve years is a long time. It makes me wonder why?"

Sarah eyed Wyatt cautiously, surprised at her own impulse to answer – he wasn't exactly a cop, and certainly not a priest.

But he *was* clearly a pragmatist, and noticed her acting skittish. She supposed she should provide an explanation.

"I guess," she said, "it's because the entire situation that night, all the drama... it was all *my* fault."

Sarah waved her hand from the Pike-house to the rest of the lake.

"Looking on it that way, you could make the case that *all* of it is."

Wyatt raised his eyes mildly. She had his interest.

Sarah hesitated, gauging his reaction.

"I was seventeen," she said, plunging forward, "and I was sleeping with my best-friend's boyfriend."

Sarah stopped there. She had never really said it right out before.

Was she looking for judgment? Absolution? Maybe it was her conscience goading her on. Or just to stamp a reason for it all after twelve years – that it was all over something as common and helpless as a teenage crush?

Wyatt waited for her to continue, even as he guided them slowly along, his all-business eyes sharp for the odd bubbling patch of lily pads or floating cadavers with hiking gear.

"I was in love," Sarah said, "the way you only are when you're seventeen. Like when you think someone thought it up just for you, and nothing quite like it had ever happened before."

Wyatt considered.

"My father," he said, "told me a crush was like a snowflake. They all might technically be unique, but there's a hell of a lot of them, and they're basically all alike. And they melt pretty fast."

Sarah considered.

"No," she said, shaking her head. "Not true here, at all."

"Burning embers after twelve-years?"

"More like core-rods," Sarah replied. "Just don't go near them."

Wyatt nodded. "Got it."

"The point is," Sarah said, "Danielle found out. And all the drama that night was directly because of that."

"Well," Wyatt allowed, "whether that's fair, the official report called it an accident."

Sarah shut her eyes.

"It... *was* an accident."

Wyatt caught the emphasis.

"You say it like you *know*. The report said, you were all drinking and didn't remember."

Wyatt was looking at her now, his face giving no tell.

But for better or worse, this was a story she had decided to tell.

"I *didn't* remember," she said. "Not at first. But... eventually, it started to come back to me."

Wyatt nodded, turning his eyes back to the water, letting Sarah speak. Taking her confession.

"I woke-up the next morning feeling *horrible*," she said. "Sleeping in the guest room."

She sighed.

"I always used the guest room when I slept-over. But that morning, Robbie was lying next to me."

She glanced quickly at Wyatt.

"Our clothes were *on*, by the way," she said.

Wyatt shrugged noncommittally.

Sarah remembered being dressed upon waking had initially been a point of relief.

Then there had been the heartbeat-throb of the hangover, and she had climbed out of bed, going down to the kitchen for water, nearly walking into the door that was left standing open, and looking outside...

And then...

Well, then she had seen something that was burned into her eyes forever – a constant afterimage flashing like a defective strobe-light in the back of her mind ever since.

Even now, as she once again stood there at the scene of it all, she felt the same near-swooning, falling-sensation, reliving the alcoholic flood of flashback-clarity images all over again.

"Robbie," she began slowly. "He didn't *mean* to kill her."

Sarah felt the sting of tears as she spoke.

"I *saw*," she said.

CHAPTER 17

"Danielle was pretty much freaking-out," Sarah said. "When Robbie tried to talk to her, she threw a bottle at his head. Deb had to pull her away."

Sarah remembered that part well – she, herself, had watched, hiding in the kitchen, with Lori sitting beside her, rapt over all the excitement.

"Unfortunately, Deb wasn't up to it," Sarah continued. "She was really more friends with *me*, and was totally not equipped to play babysitter once Danielle got one of her wildings on. After about ten minutes, she came back in and reported Danielle had simply run off into the woods."

Sarah recalled Deb was also sporting a fat-lip, roughly the size of Danielle's class ring.

"I think she was headed to the hot-springs," Deb had scowled, firmly wiping her hands of it.

"You just let her go off into the woods?" Robbie objected.

"Yeah," Deb replied, pointing to her swelling lip. "I tried to stop her and she punched me."

Deb waved a middle-finger over her shoulder.

"*Bitch.*"

Sarah had heard more than one person describe Danielle exactly the same way. It was actually a hard point to argue.

Although, to shame the Devil, the truth was, Sarah was the one who betrayed their friendship.

She debated heading up to the hot-springs, but knew she was the last person Danielle would be willing to talk to.

Instead, she had gotten drunk.

Wyatt's account on the police-report was correct – when she woke-up, the next morning, with her skull on fire, and her eyes too bloody to see, the night had been a complete blank.

She actually hadn't intended to get quite *that* drunk.

After Danielle ran off, and Lori had gone to bed – *protesting* – Sarah found herself third-wheel as Kenny and Deb suddenly seemed to have found eyes for each other, and clearly didn't want her around.

"That was why *they* didn't hear anything after midnight," Sarah said, archly. "They were up in Mr. Pike's bedroom, with the stereo on."

Sarah herself had simply retreated to the couch and her interrupted horror-movies, sipping lightly at the bottle until she fell asleep.

"Something woke me in the middle of the night,"

Sarah shut her eyes – this was a story she had never told.

"Danielle was back. She and Robbie were out on the porch and they were fighting. And I mean *fighting*. She was hitting him. *Hard*. He was covering-up, trying to talk to her."

Sarah let out a breath.

"I was watching out the window, and I just about decided to step in, when he finally hit her back."

Sarah shrugged.

"That was it. She fell and hit her head on the concrete. And it killed her. Just that easy."

She felt the sting of old tears.

"I went out on the deck, and he was bent over her, crying. He was looking up at me, and he kept on saying, 'I didn't *mean* it!'"

She wiped at her eyes, frustrated.

"I *knew* he didn't mean it. I *saw*. He just hit her and she fell. She was attacking *him!*"

Sarah glanced at Wyatt, whose face remained mild – nothing more on his mind than guiding the boat.

"He panicked," Sarah said. "Robbie was a kid just like the rest of us. And he behaved like a kid who made a mess and tried to hide it."

Now the sting of tears stopped. The only way to tell this part was with cauterized nerves. So she sucked it up, and spit it out.

"He took her out to the piranha pond and he threw her in."

Sarah bowed her head.

"I didn't do anything to stop him. And I didn't say anything later on. And in the morning, I didn't even remember. I just came out and saw them. Her and Mr. Pike."

Wyatt nodded.

"The report said he was still in his business clothes," Wyatt said. "They think he was trying to fish her out and slipped in himself."

"I hid Lori away after I found them," Sarah said. "I wouldn't let her go outside. But she saw the emergency-chopper and the paramedics, and she knew well enough where the piranha-pond was."

Sarah choked on her voice.

"When they pulled him out, she asked me, 'Is that my *Dad?*'"

She made sure to say that part straight-out and brutal.

"So," Wyatt asked, "whereabouts would you say you had this memory relapse?"

Sarah paused. Withholding judgment? Or confirming guilt?

"I was back home in Lewiston," she said. "Everyone else lived in town. They pretty much let the rest of us go. I mean, they never really *arrested* any of us. But they kept after Robbie a little longer. They knew there was a fight. And they knew it was over catching him with me."

"Makes sense they'd look at the boyfriend," Wyatt allowed. "And, it seems that they would have been right."

"It was about three weeks later, when I heard they let him go." Sarah shrugged. "And then it all just came back to me."

Sarah remembered *that* moment well. Up to that point, she had been dealing with a tragedy, but her conscience had been clear.

Then the memories came flooding back...

"None of us kids ever really saw each other afterward," Sarah said. "I never talked to Robbie again." She half-laughed. "My dad would have freaked."

But she held up her hand.

"Don't get me wrong," she said. "By then I was *over* it. But I couldn't bring myself to send him to jail. It wouldn't bring Danielle back. It wouldn't help her folks. I didn't want to destroy his life on top of it all."

"Well," Wyatt said, "he made it to jail anyway. Things have a way of taking care of themselves. I think, they call it karma."

Sarah looked at him sideways, as he turned the boat back around, leaving the Pike-property behind.

"I take it," she said, "you think I've got some karma coming to *me*, then?"

Wyatt shrugged.

"I'm guessing *you* think so," he replied. "Why else would you tell me that story? You want me to tell you it's alright? Well, of course it isn't. And if I were a cop, I'd probably arrest both you *and* Mr. Ray."

"But you're not a cop," Sarah said.

"Nope. But maybe you're hoping I'll pass this little story along to the real cops, so you don't have to." Wyatt shrugged. "Maybe you're not as over this guy as you say. And that's causing you to act against your conscience."

Sarah raised an eyebrow.

"A little psychology, Officer Wyatt?"

"I dabble," he replied. "But like I said, I'm not a cop. Until you break a gaming law, your personal life is none of my business. And if you want to inform the authorities of what you told me, you should do it yourself."

Sarah was pretty certain such a conversation would put Robbie – fresh out of prison – right back behind bars, very quickly.

She wasn't certain about herself. She fell silent, as Wyatt steered them towards her lagoon.

Then Wyatt brought them to an abrupt stop.

"Well," he said. "What have we here?"'

As they approached Sarah's lagoon, they saw a boat floating discreetly off to one side, but still in sight of the house.

Its lights were off and it appeared to be anchored.

"That's Norman's boat," Wyatt said, and flashed his spotlight.

The face staring back over the bow was Robbie.

Wyatt kept the light on him as they approached. Robbie covered his eyes.

"Mr. Ray," Wyatt said. "What are you doing out here? Fish and Game business?"

Robbie frowned, not answering. Then his eyes turned to Sarah.

"I saw you today," he said.

Those same smoldering eyes. A little scary now.

"That's what I'm doing, okay?" Robbie said. "I wanted to see you. And I've been sitting here for an hour, too chickenshit to do it."

"I hope you're doing alright, Robbie," Sarah said, noncommittally, offering nothing else.

"Mr. Ray," Wyatt said, "I'm glad I caught you. Since Norman seems to have abdicated his responsibilities tomorrow, that means you're going to be on lake-patrol."

"What do you mean 'patrol'?"

"We need to keep people off the lake. Probably, for at least the next few days. You'll need to be out early. Right out in the pre-dawn, before the fishermen get there."

Wyatt checked his watch.

"So, you've got an early morning. You should be headed off for bed."

Robbie didn't quite dare scowl.

Sarah faded back, resolutely silent.

"And," Wyatt added, "if I think you're stalking this young lady, I'll speak to your parole-board and have your work-release terminated. That means back to prison."

Robbie's face darkened, but he was bound to inmate-obedience.

"Get on home, now," Wyatt said.

Robbie nodded sullenly to Sarah.

"It was good to see you," he said.

"You too, Robbie," Sarah replied, carefully neutral.

He spared Wyatt one last glare before starting his boat, turning out of the lagoon towards the main lake.

Wyatt steered them back to the waiting dock. At the sound of their boat, the kitchen-blinds pulled up and Sarah saw Deb looking out.

Sarah waved. Deb waved doubtfully back.

There was a bump as Wyatt guided them through the water-lilies and into the dock. He extended his hand to help her with the ladder.

Sarah recalled her own less-than-charitable thoughts on thuggish professions. Perhaps in a world of thugs, there was a place for thug-like counter-measures. She glanced back the direction Robbie had disappeared.

"Thank you for that," she said. "I've been thanking you a lot, just lately."

Wyatt shrugged.

"Wanna make-out?" he asked, dead-pan.

Sarah's jaw dropped, before he shook his head.

"Sorry," he said. "Joke."

Sarah smacked him on the arm, before she caught herself, running quick self-psychology – was this like the girl who hits the boy she has a crush on?

Was that what she was doing?

Or was she just hitting him?

"I'm not planning on telling anybody what you told me tonight," Wyatt said. "But you obviously wanted me to know, so I'm going to remember."

She took his offered hand, being tender with her still-sore rump, as she climbed the ladder to the dock.

"You have my number," Wyatt said. "Keep me posted."

"I will."

"Try not to fall in again."

Sarah smiled.

"I'll try."

Wyatt pushed his boat back out into the lagoon, starting the motor, and turning back towards the lake. He quickly became indistinct in the shroud of evening mist.

Behind her, Kenny joined Deb at the window.

Sarah watched until Wyatt's lights disappeared, before she turned back to the house.

She had an itinerary to plan, and she figured tomorrow was going to be a busy day.

As it turned out, she wasn't wrong.

CHAPTER 18

As evening settled in, Lori sat apart from the others.

Adrienne and Dana's overnight ordeal earned them appropriate pampering – even from the normally impatient Pamela, who set them up in the living room with heated-blankets and even served them dinner.

There was dutiful reverence over Jack Burrell, although no one really knew what exactly to say on a few hours' acquaintance. Josh and Paul had never even seen him with his skin on.

But once proper respects were paid, the party began to relax.

Lori had seen a lot of parties – this one was developing like a wake, starting low-key and moody.

Josh and Paul had come well-stocked, and grabbed several cases, along with a couple fifths, from their boat. Lori guessed, from the look of them, that was keeping it light.

It was, after all, something she had a little too much experience with.

In point of fact, it was like a crutch that was practically being whacked across her head tonight.

Lori wondered mildly if she would succumb or not – it was still too early to tell. Her world was finally collapsing the rest of the way.

Paul was making drinks. He poured soda with a double shot over ice and handed it to Lori, who sat perched like a cat in what had once been her father's easy-chair.

Pamela stepped up discreetly, took the glass from Lori's hand, handing her a cup of coffee, and waggling a finger.

"Don't go diving off the wagon just yet," the old nurse admonished.

Lori shrugged, sipping the coffee instead. Pamela smiled, patting an encouraging hand on her shoulder.

As she retreated to the kitchen, Pamela tossed the drink in a swig.

"*Damn*, woman," Henry objected over the dishes as Pamela handed him the empty glass. "Ever think of sharing?"

Meanwhile, Adrienne, who had just spent the night in a tree, and was losing her job along with that fall's tuition payment, had now been told the hot-tub wasn't working.

Adrienne, apparently not quite aware of who Lori actually was, announced she was going to, "sue the owner just for that alone."

Lori arrowed a narrow eye through the back of Adrienne's head, although the truth was, she didn't know whether to be more angry or ashamed. For all Adrienne's woes about college, Lori was looking at losing her home and maybe going to jail.

On the other hand, Adrienne *did* see a guy eaten by piranhas, and had to spend a night in a tree. *Aaaand* those piranha probably came, at least originally, from right here where Lori had grown up, raised by her own father.

She glanced down at her phone, and Sarah's number.

Lori still hadn't called.

Was it just shame? The same reason she said nothing to Adrienne? Was she just hiding her head in the sand?

That was one of the benefits of having no one left who really knew you – nobody remembered what you used to be, or how far you'd fallen. It was easier to hide.

Lori remembered that night a dozen years ago, too. She also remembered the morning after. And while it may not have been obvious to the adults around her, Lori, as a kid, herself, saw how Sarah had run away.

A psychiatrist might have suggested Lori felt abandoned, even blamed Sarah, although no doctor ever had, because Lori never mentioned it to any of them.

She put her phone back in her pocket.

Sipping her coffee, Lori watched the high-octanes take effect around her. She knew the party-stages well, and first, was the initial hurry to get reckless.

Adrienne was holding point, cuddling with Josh. Dana, more reserved, paired-off with Paul by default – although no decisions were made yet, because Anne and Amy both still hovered.

Donna retired early, uninterested in high-octanes or high-testosterone. Yesterday, her missionary-jargon had annoyed Lori the most, but today, out of all the councilors, she seemed the least self-concerned that the camp appeared to be folding.

Paul, not satisfied with just three girls circling, took one last fly-by past Lori – noticing the coffee cup in her hand, he held up his whiskey bottle.

"Refresher?"

Lori smiled, shaking her head, *no*.

"Just give it to me this time," Henry said, shutting off the lights in the kitchen. "The wife gets mean when she drinks."

Paul got the point when Pamela took a swat at his head – a good smart rap – as she snatched the bottle from his hand.

"Don't you go corrupting her," the old nurse warned, offering-up another smart swat before turning heel, and marching out of the room down the hall.

Paul stared at his empty hand and then at Henry, who shrugged, before simply following his wife, who was already tipping the bottle.

Dave leaned in around ten.

"Just doing a head-check," he said. "After last night, I want to make sure everyone's accounted for."

Adrienne held up her glass.

"And still counting," she said, with just the barest touch of a slur.

Dave smiled.

"Try to keep it down," he said. He glanced over to where Lori sat unobtrusively by the window.

"We should hear sometime tomorrow what the immediate future is for the camp," he said. "We'll call a meeting and talk about it then."

Anne faded off to bed an hour later. Amy hung-on a little bit longer – Paul seemed to have eyes for Dana, but Amy thought she might conceivably throw him back.

Although, Dana *was* the first to ask about the hot-tub.

"Actually," Lori volunteered, from her unobtrusive perch by the window, "we have one. But it's not working. I think it's the one thing the construction crew didn't fix."

The group fell briefly silent at Lori's abrupt contribution.

"Well," Josh said, running a stealthy hand up Adrienne's bare leg, "it's a nice night for a swim."

Adrienne slapped his chest.

"*Ugghh!* Don't even *say* that. That's not funny."

Dana likewise groaned aloud. Amy, who hadn't seen the leftovers of Jack, simply smiled politely.

"On the other hand," Paul said, "there *are* the hot-springs, just up the way from here. I used to go there when I was in high school."

Adrienne leaned forward, interested.

"I've heard of those. How far are they?"

Paul shrugged.

"Just a short hike. Maybe a mile."

Adrienne was sold, climbing out of Josh's lap, pulling him to his feet.

"I wanna go!" she demanded. Josh rose with her agreeably enough.

Paul nodded to Dana and Amy, who both looked less certain.

"Yeah," Dana said. "A walk in the woods at a remote summer camp in the middle of the night. What could go wrong?"

But that only added spice for Adrienne.

"Oh, we *gotta* go, now," she said, laughing, running to the laundry and returning with a handful of beach towels.

Dana sighed, glancing at Amy beside her.

"Why not?" she asked.

"Well," Lori offered, mildly, "there's bears."

She smiled sweetly as they all looked back at her again, still having no idea who she was.

"Bears," Lori said again, nodding. "Big ones. Grizzlies."

"Okay," Amy said, "*that's* why not." She tossed her towel back to Adrienne, and waved to the group. "*I'm* calling it a night."

Dana made a move as if to follow, but Adrienne grabbed her arm.

"Come on, don't be chicken."

"Bears," Dana said, nervously.

"And cougar," Lori added.

Dana looked unhappy, but allowed herself to be tugged and cajoled out the door. Josh produced a flashlight, pulling Adrienne under his arm. Resigned, Dana tucked herself under Paul's wing, as well, following the other two around the back of the house, up into the dark.

At first, Lori could see their flashlight bumping around among the trees, going up the hill. Then the light disappeared in the mist.

Lori now sat alone in her own living room for the first time since she'd been back.

Her eyes turned to one of the open bottles Paul and Josh had left on her table.

It reminded her of that night twelve years ago, that same table with sticky shot-glasses scattered all about it. At twelve, it wasn't the first time Lori had drunk alcohol – not even the first time she'd drank a *lot*, but it was her first heavy-drinking with hard liquor, and she remembered practically gagging with the taste of her father's whiskey.

In the middle of the night, she had woken-up sick. She had been roused by someone shouting – probably a good thing, because she didn't throw-up in her sleep.

There had been voices – one of them was Robbie, unintelligible, sounding defensive, and then a girl, loud and angry, "They'll never believe you!"

And then, a wave of vertigo had hit her – she had rushed to the bathroom and began throwing-up.

That lasted nearly an hour, after which, she curled around the toilet for another thirty-minutes, swearing she could feel the actual rotation of the Earth, before finally making her way back to her bedroom.

The next thing she knew, it was morning and there were emergency vehicles on her lawn.

When she'd gotten up, Sarah met her at her bedroom door, grabbing hold of her, and telling her not to go outside.

But of course, she did.

She had to see. She had to *know*.

It was twelve years ago, but Lori could look out on the grounds and see it clearly as if it were happening that very moment.

Because, as it turned out, it was still happening – the events set in motion that night never stopped – the brooms kept marching.

Lori shut her eyes. She was *so* tired.

Her eyelids began to flutter into a doze.

When Lori started back awake enough to make her way to bed, the hot-springs party had been gone nearly an hour.

No one noticed them missing until morning.

CHAPTER 19

Fish don't think. They are extremely primitive creatures, with no cognitive function to speak of. Their actions are strictly instinctual.

This does not mean they are not capable of complex or adaptive behavior.

Lake Perdition was the last place a population of piranha should even survive, let alone thrive.

But they followed the most simple of instincts, the way a flower will bend towards light, these fish gravitated to heat.

The sinkholes under the lake were always a geological feature of the region, and recent seismic activity had opened up even more – the 'hot-spots' highlighted on the satellites, connecting the flooded caverns below.

Like bats streaming from the mouth of a cave at sunset, when the first crack of dawn touched the morning mist on Lake Perdition, the fish came flooding out of the cracks in the lake floor.

Seen from above, it would have appeared like a shimmering ripple under the surface as, all over the lake, shoals of black piranha, numbering in the hundreds and averaging over five pounds, poured from the underwater vents like billowing clouds.

Feeding time.

But in recent weeks, food had grown more and more scarce.

The fish were growing more and more desperate.

Sarah was right on two counts.

They *were* starving.

And they *had* indeed arrived at a very dangerous point.

Today, with the dawn, came the first belligerent, growling sounds of boat motors echoing across the rocky basin.

The fish shoaled tighter together in response to the threat.

Ready to swarm.

CHAPTER 20

It was still pre-dawn when Sarah woke to a beeping phone. When she checked, blurry-eyed, there was a message from Wyatt.

"This is the bullshit I'm already dealing with."

He attached a link to the lake's website comment page.

"Wyatt's shutting down the lake because of piranha? Are you shitting me?"

"Is he nuts?"

"I've seen bears gnaw a skeleton to the bone."

"So post a no-swimming sign and let us fish."

Wyatt called a half-hour later, while Sarah gathered with Kenny and Deb around coffee.

"Put me on speaker," he instructed.

Kenny rolled his eyes, as Sarah set her phone in the center of the table.

"Morning folks," Wyatt said. "Just a head's-up. I found three campsites last night. I threatened them with fines, but gave them a pass if they left first thing this morning. One group actually kayaked. *Rubber* kayaks, no less. I showed them pictures of the cadavers from the morgue, and told them I'd send Norman out with the water-taxi to pick them up. You can tell anyone you see the same thing."

"Got it," Sarah said. "We'll keep in touch."

She picked her phone off the table.

"That control-freak SOB is probably enjoying this," Kenny remarked.

Sarah looked at him, pained, waggling the phone in her hand.

"I'm still here, dumbshit," Wyatt said.

There was a moment of awkward silence – Sarah could just *see* Wyatt scowl.

"Anyway," Wyatt continued, "like I said last night, if you see anybody, just show them the bulletin, tell them they're subject to fines, blah-blah. I don't really care if they just get off the lake.

"And by the way, Mitchell," he added, "people hate guys like me, but I'm just enforcing the rules guys like you write."

This time, there was the definitive beep of a disconnected line.

"I believe he has a point, dear," Deb said, nudging him.

Kenny shrugged, frowning.

"I suppose the world needs thugs too," he said.

"You know," Sarah said, "he's not such a bad guy."

Kenny glanced at her sideways.

"You are literally the first person I've ever heard say that," he said.

Sarah was surprised to find herself a little angry. She thought about mentioning the scene with Robbie. Instead, she simply shrugged.

"What can I say? He saved my life."

Kenny turned away, a bit shame-faced. Deb eyed him quizzically.

"Does that bother you, that they get along?"

"No," Kenny said. "I mean..."

He waved his hand.

"Forget it," he said, deliberately turning his attention to the map on Sarah's computer screen. "Where are we today?"

Sarah ran the mouse along a series of red highlights.

"Same as yesterday. I'll take my little outboard down the north shore. You two keep to the south. You've got my folks' boat again. Just check as many spots as you can. They're definitely breeding, so collect eggs where you find them.

"And," she said, "be *careful* out there."

CHAPTER 21

Lori got an early call too – a knock at the door.

It was still dark, but her father's lawyers were on New York time.

When she answered, she found Dave standing there. Lori always half-expected him to appear at her door one night, maybe loosened up with a few beers.

But tonight, he simply looked grim, even apologetic.

"I just got official word," he said. "The bank's pulling the funding. The lawyers have officially terminated the camp."

Lori sighed. Not a surprise.

"I'll tell everyone else at breakfast," Dave said, "but I thought you should know first."

Lori actually could have waited.

"All employees," Dave said, "will be compensated through the end of the work-day as of yesterday, and will be expected to vacate the property by the end of today." He shrugged. "I've already got the water-taxi coming to pick everyone up this morning."

"What about me?" Lori asked. "Am I an employee? Am I expected to vacate too?"

"As of now," Dave said, "you are still the owner and may stay on the property as long as that remains the case."

But Lori knew that might not be very long.

"If the bank forecloses," Dave said, "at that time, you would likely be required to move out."

"Of course."

"And unfortunately," Dave continued, "there is nothing preventing families of anyone who has been injured from suing the estate."

Lori leaned against her door.

"Anything else?"

"No response yet from the DA's office about your probation commitment. But it does represent a failure to meet your obligations."

Dave shrugged helplessly.

"I'm sorry," he said.

His eyes looked genuinely sympathetic. He reached out a hand to touch her shoulder, but Lori jerked quickly away.

Dave stepped back as if he hadn't noticed.

"I'll see you at breakfast," he said, and turned back down the hall to his room. Lori shut the door behind him and sat down on her bed.

Well. That was it, then.

She looked around her house, wondering how long she really had. Months? Weeks?

That was to say nothing of what the DA's office might have to say.

Her head throbbed.

She'd stayed vigilantly perched on the wagon as of last night, but this sure *felt* like a hangover.

In fact, she chose to treat it that way, taking two aspirin and climbing back into bed.

She must have fallen asleep for at least a couple more hours because the next thing she knew, Dave was back, knocking at her door, to tell her Adrienne and Dana never returned from the hot-springs last night, and Josh and Paul were missing with them.

CHAPTER 22

Robbie had camped on the boat last night.

After Wyatt ordered him off, Robbie retreated north of Devil's Island, figuring the game warden would take the safer, southern route on his way back to town.

Robbie waited, hiding in the shadows of the rocks, until he saw Wyatt's boat pass. Then Robbie circled back around to the Boneyard and tied-off to a tree.

Sarah's cove was already indistinct in the evening mist, and soon it would fade away altogether, like some mystical lagoon that only appeared on this plane once every dozen years.

Robbie had Sarah's number typed-up on his phone. It had been easy enough to get – he just called her office, told them he was with Fish and Game, and he needed her field-number.

All true.

Of course, if he called, a negative reaction on her part might very well land him back in prison. Wyatt was never known to bluff.

But there remained unfinished business – air to be cleared, conversations yet-to-be-had – and long-denied, goddammit.

His finger hovered over the call button.

What was it really worth?

Moreover, what was his response truly likely to be?

Kenny and Deb were staying with her, remember. It might be different if she were alone.

He stared at the number for a long time before putting the phone back into his pocket, spreading his bedroll, and letting the boat rock him under the starless sky.

All through the night, hoots, howls, and whistling wind blended with haunting dreams.

The next thing he was aware of was blinking awake to his ringing phone. It was still dark, well before dawn.

Robbie grunted, his blurry eyes reading *Hayden M. Wyatt* as incoming-caller.

Grumbling, Robbie tapped the line.

"Hello?"

"You up, Mr. Ray?" Wyatt asked brightly, with drill-sergeant enthusiasm. "I'm expecting you out on the lake before any fishermen are."

Wyatt glanced around at the water, balancing himself on the rocking boat.

"Not a problem," Robbie said.

"I want you to take the north shore, west of the old hatchery," Wyatt said. "You're not as likely to run into anyone out there, but the area needs to be covered. I'll be expecting you to check-in, understand?"

Robbie's eyes narrowed. He *wouldn't* be checking in, just because of *that*. He wondered if that would earn him a reprimand with his probation officer.

"Otherwise, I'll be checking with *you*," Wyatt finished.

Robbie bit down his initial reply.

"Anything else?"

"Don't fall in," Wyatt said, and hung up.

Muttering under his breath, Robbie started the motor. The hatchery was almost fifteen miles back, which would take forty-five minutes in the dark.

It would probably be a good idea to be far away from Sarah's cove before anyone spotted his boat.

He looked down at her number again, wondering if he was going to be able to let it go. After all this time, he should *want* to.

But, boy, when he had seen her yesterday...?

Everything came back.

Three years in jail should have finally dried it out of him. Instead, that pit in his gut seemed to have fermented, maybe metastasized.

The rising sun was beginning to glaze the drifting mist – it was a red sky *every* morning on Lake Perdition. Robbie slowed his boat cautiously.

Just around the bend, were the crypt-like shadows of the old hatchery, bordering the south shore. At the fork beyond, Robbie veered into the northwest lochs – a section of the lake Norman described as 'best ignored'. They were heavily-hooded in trees, and got a lot of snow-melt – when the lake had recreation, it was dangerously cold for swimming, and even the trout preferred the warmer water out in the main lake.

Wyatt had given no specific instructions, beyond patrolling for wayward fishermen, so Robbie simply trolled along the shore. Normally, there were worse jobs than just cruising around in a boat all day.

But today, that also gave him time to think. That was never a good start.

He glanced back the direction he'd come, wondering if Sarah was out on the lake yet.

And as his attention briefly wavered, something bumped under the hull of his boat, thumping beneath his feet, like a large branch, or medium-sized log.

"Damn," he muttered, slowing the boat to a stop, and examining the hull for damage. No marks. Then he looked back after what he had hit.

There was a floating mass in the water behind him. It was a moment before he realized what he was seeing.

"Oh, *Jesus*," he breathed.

It was a human skeleton, stripped clean of flesh, still adorned in hiking gear.

Then there was another bump under the boat.

He looked over the side as another mass bobbed-up from underneath.

"What the *hell...?*"

He realized there were several floating bodies, clumped together, in the water ahead.

One of them had its head propped up out of the water, like a branch on a dead log – the long strands of remaining hair suggested it was once a woman – now the face was a fleshless rictus, with dark hollowed-out eye-sockets that stared vacantly through the ghostly white mist.

Robbie knew well enough what had happened to them. He'd seen it before.

He tapped his phone – Sarah's number was still onscreen.

Robbie looked at the corpses floating around his boat.

The chickens, so to speak, had come home to roost.

He touched Sarah's number and waited for the ring, not sure what he was going to say – the first words they would speak in nearly a dozen years.

"Hello?" Sarah answered quizzically, at the '*Fish and Game*' caller-ID on her work-number.

"Hi Sarah, this is Robbie."

He allowed for one moment of dead silence on the other end. He would be lying if a small, mean part of him didn't enjoy it.

"Why are you calling me, Robbie?" Sarah asked, tonelessly. "You remember what Wyatt told you."

Robbie suppressed a slow-burn.

"I remember," he said. "But I just found a bunch of dead bodies. I think it's your missing hikers."

Another beat of silence.

"Where?" Sarah asked.

"The northwest lochs," he said. "They're all eaten right to the bone."

He knew that was something they *both* had seen before.

"I thought you'd want to know," Robbie said.

CHAPTER 23

The first person bit by a fish that day was from one of the campsites Wyatt had already rousted the night before.

Charlie and Bernie Mullins were Paul and Josh's cousins, and had intended to meet-up the day before. That is, until Josh called to tell them about a dead guy, and two hot girls up a tree.

They also warned that Wyatt was on the prowl, so when the game warden had, indeed, caught them camping along the south bank – slipping up on them, just as silent and sneaky as that SOB always did – they already knew perfectly well that the lake was closed and why.

Of course, it was prudent to play dumb as Wyatt read them the list of fines they'd accrued just being there. But then, rather uncharacteristically, he offered them the option of simply leaving.

Wyatt pointed to the fancy iPhone in Charlie's pocket.

"All this is posted. I don't suppose you ever check the lake website?"

Charlie exchanged innocent looks with Bernie.

"Out of here, first light tomorrow," Wyatt said, as he pushed his boat back onto the lake.

So they camped out the night, waiting to hear from Josh and Paul, who last texted that the tree-girls had taken them home.

Josh sent a selfie with an armful of bikini-clad maidens, all holding up drink glasses.

Charlie hadn't heard from them since.

"Probably have to wait until tomorrow to get *that* story," Bernie remarked.

"He'd never think of inviting his cousins over, would he?" Charlie returned archly.

Bernie shrugged.

"To be fair, *I* wouldn't call us, either."

Charlie conceded the point.

All across the lake, the nightly whippoorwill calls of the night-creatures began to echo. It used to give him the creeps when he was a kid.

Still did, actually, although Jack Daniels helped – they had just finished their first bottle, and Charlie pitched it out into the lake, skipping the empty fifth like a rock, until it disappeared into the fog.

He peered out into the shifting indistinct darkness.

"You think there really are *piranha* out there?" he asked.

Bernie shrugged.

"Josh said that guy was eaten to the bone."

Yet, repeated casts from the shore yielded nothing except a few broken leaders caught in the rocks.

The rest of the evening wasn't much more than sitting and drinking by the fire. In the morning, they were frankly happy enough to leave.

Rumor had it that this was a dead lake anyway. They were already lucky not to be hauled-in by Wyatt.

After sleeping-off the night's drink, they broke camp. With one last text to Josh, who still hadn't answered, they loaded their boat, pushed out into the lake, and headed for home.

Everything would have been fine, except, once out in deeper water, Charlie decided to toss his line in the water one last time, attaching a jig-style lure with a sturdy length of wire.

This time, in the morning daylight, the line was hit immediately.

"*Holy...!*" Charlie blurted, "this is *big*!"

He jerked the hook tight and began to reel.

"Damn," Bernie said, excited, "look at him fight!"

The rod jerked in Charlie's hands like he'd hooked a marlin. But then, just as he was drawing his catch near the boat, the line suddenly went doubly haywire.

"Jesus!" Bernie exclaimed, as they could see half-a-dozen large black shapes splashing at the end of the line – whatever was on the hook was now being hit by its fellows. Charlie reeled as fast as he could.

When he yanked the line out of the water, the fish he'd hooked was gutted and half-eaten, but it was still gasping over the wicked jig-hooks sunk deep into an even wickeder set of jaws.

"Will you look at that?" Bernie said, amazed, as Charlie dangled his catch over the railing into the boat.

Charlie had seen *little* piranha – a friend had one in a fish-tank. But this thing had to be seven pounds – at least, it was before its friends got at it.

"Those are some mean-looking teeth," Bernie remarked.

Charlie reached for the line, intending to drop the still-twitching, half-dead fish to the floor, but the thing suddenly spasmed wildly, the lunging jaws snapping at his reaching hand, and bit both his index and middle-finger completely off.

The fish kicked, tearing itself loose from the hook, flopping back over the side into the water, where it was instantly set-upon by its fellows, and devoured in seconds.

Charlie stared disbelievingly at his own spurting blood. His fingers had been chopped as clean as a carrot-cutter, before he could even jerk away.

"Oh, my dear *Jesus*," he wailed, clutching his hands together. Wide-eyed, Bernie bent beside him.

A moment later, they both were startled as a boat-horn sounded. They looked to see Wyatt's boat sidling-up, smooth and quiet stalker that he was.

"For crying out loud, Mullins!" Wyatt hollered over. "I told you to be gone at first light"

His face ashen, Charlie turned, and Wyatt could see his injured hand.

Wyatt cursed, bringing his boat up beside them, already opening his first-aid kit.

With the quickness of a field medic, Wyatt lashed the two boats together and snatched-up Charlie's wounded hand, wrapping enough tape and gauze to quell the bleeding.

"Damn," he remarked, "that sonofabitch got you good."

He nodded to Bernie.

"You think you can get back to town okay? Get him to a hospital?"

Bernie nodded numbly.

"Then get going," Wyatt said. "And if you happen to see anyone else, tell them to get the hell off the lake."

He pulled the lashing, separating the boats.

As he pushed away, his phone rang in his pocket. Wyatt frowned as he saw the number, and answered the call.

"Sarah?"

"Wyatt? We've got more bodies. I think it's your hikers."

"Where?"

Sarah sounded hesitant.

"Well..., actually, it was Robbie that found them. He called me. He found five bodies, all on the northwest lochs, past the hatchery."

"Robbie called *you*?"

"He got my number from my office. Wyatt... I need to go out there but..."

She sounded embarrassed.

"Will you meet me there?"

Wyatt nodded as he spoke.

"Right now, I'm on the south shore, probably about ten miles out," he said. "But I'll be there."

"Thank you."

Wyatt turned to Charlie and Bernie, who seemed to be hanging on his call.

"What did I say?" he barked. "You got fifteen miles by boat. Now *get!*"

Bernie started up the motor, turning the boat back towards town.

Wyatt looked after them, shaking his head. Damned fools were lucky he checked on them – ol' Charlie might've bled to death.

The game warden sighed as he watched the two fishermen motoring off. He supposed he should count his blessings. So far, the lake had been mostly empty of fishermen. He'd called on all three camps he'd rousted the night before. The first group was already packed and leaving, mostly cordial.

The second were the kayakers, still waiting on the water-taxi. Wyatt assured them he'd already seen Norman firing up the old stern-wheeler on his way out that morning.

Norm had tooted his horn as Wyatt passed by. Wyatt had called him, waiting nine rings before Norman answered.

"You seen anybody out?" Wyatt asked.

"Not on the lake. A few people showed up at the dock. The town sheriff has a deputy there, turning them away from the lake."

"You got the call about the Pike-house?"

"Yep," Norman said. "Picking-up your kayakers first. Then off to the Pike-house. I guess they're all going home. The lake's shutting down all over again."

Wyatt heard regret in the old man's voice. As an enforcer, he was sympathetic, but he didn't know what else to do.

"I should have everyone picked-up by mid-morning," Norman said.

"Keep south of Devil's Island," Wyatt warned. "And stay clear of Purgatory Cove. The last thing we need is you dragging that boat over one of those rocks."

Norman agreed. That had been well over an hour ago. Hopefully, he'd made his pick-ups, and was on his way back.

Wyatt focused his binoculars briefly after Charlie and Bernie, making sure they were on their way. The water-taxi was not yet visible.

So far, the lake itself was barren. Today, that was a good thing.

Wyatt checked his watch. Sarah would be waiting for him.

He turned his boat towards the northwest shore.

CHAPTER 24

Kenny and Deb also stumbled onto an errant fishing boat, tucked into a little cove a mile west of the hatchery – right where Sarah sent them to check out one of the largest hot-spots along the south shore.

This boat contained a pair of large hominids, round-chested and bearded, who appeared displeased at being disturbed.

Kenny glanced nervously at Deb, who only shrugged.

"Hey, fellas," Kenny called over. "Gotta pass on the word. The lake's closed. Fishing season's off."

The two men exchanged shrugs.

"Well, you know we were already out here," the first one said, waving his hand dismissively.

Kenny smarted a bit.

"Actually, guys," he said, keeping his voice even, "it's dangerous. There's..."

"Piranha," the second man said. "Yeah, we know."

He held up his creel, filled with big five and six pounders.

"We figure a fish is a fish. We're eaten' somethin' tonight."

The first man held up his own catch.

"And these things will bite at anything."

Kenny wondered if any of those fish might have pieces of Artie Langstrom or Jack Burrell still digesting inside them.

"Fish-fry," Deb remarked, "Wyatt wasn't wrong."

"Sorry, guys," Kenny said, "but the lake's closed. You're going to have to leave."

The two of them bristled.

"And who the hell are you?"

"I'm with Fish and Game," Kenny retorted.

That seemed to leave them unimpressed.

"Hayden Wyatt," Deb added, "is out on the lake today. He told us to call if we had problems."

Now the two men exchanged glances.

The second man set his creel back in the boat.

"I'm keeping these," he said defiantly.

Kenny made a dismissive wave with his hand. "Just get going."

The two fishermen glared balefully, but they pulled in their poles, started up their motor and took off, withholding any further remarks.

Kenny stood in the boat, staring after them, until they turned south out of the cove, towards town.

"Well," Deb said archly, "look at *you*."

"What?"

"Are you an alpha-male now?"

"What does that mean?"

"It means Sarah likes manly-types, just like Danielle did. And she doesn't see you like that. Just like Danielle didn't."

Kenny frowned.

"But Wyatt fits the bill, doesn't he? That's why you didn't like it when I name-dropped him. Because those guys weren't going to leave because *you* told them to."

"I asked Sarah on *one* date in high school," Kenny said patiently. "Twelve *years* ago."

"Yeah," Deb responded quickly. "And we've been together ever since. But we still aren't married. Could it be, one of us is holding out for a better deal?"

Kenny's temper sparked.

"Alright, Deb," he said, "*stop* it."

Deb's eyes narrowed, but she waved it off.

"Fine," she said, turning to the surrounding lagoon. She pointed to the lilies floating along the shore.

"Those two guys probably had a dozen fish between them," she said. "They're definitely here."

Kenny held up one hand.

"Wait," he said, "listen."

There was the loud liquid belch of a vent from below. Sure enough, right in the midst of the lilies, they could see a steady bubbling, just like a giant bullfrog.

"I think we can safely confirm a hot-spot," Deb said. "Check those stalks for eggs."

Kenny steered into the patch of floating leaves.

Deb nodded to the water.

"You do the honors," she said.

Kenny looked cautiously over the railing. Grabbing a boat hook, he dipped it over the side, hooking the stalk of one of the nearest lilies.

The hook was nearly jarred out of his hand as something hit it from below. Kenny started backwards, splashing water, yanking the hook loose, along with the tattered plant stalk. Deb shrieked as water splashed her face.

Kenny dropped the plant-stalk into the boat. The surface of the water roiled.

"Jeez, they're being aggressive," Kenny said, staring wide-eyed over the railing.

"They're just watching out for their babies," Deb said. "Look here."

She ran her finger along the stalk, which was gelled with eggs.

Deb frowned.

"A lot of these look like they're dead," she said. "But some of these others might still be viable." She turned the stalk in her hands. "Piranha already reproduce in high numbers to account for high-infant-mortality. They lay a lot of eggs. It looks to me like this outer layer of dead eggs is providing insulation for those at the center."

Deb nodded speculatively.

"I'm guessing that if you tossed these stalks in the Amazon basin, or anything resembling their natural environment, you'd get a few of these eggs hatching. Not a lot, from what I see here, but you take away the predators, you might actually have a positive survival rate."

Kenny scraped at the gelled eggs doubtfully.

"That still doesn't account for their numbers. Or size. This isn't a struggling, barely-subsisting population."

Deb shrugged.

"Bigger nests somewhere else? Maybe just all of them together?"

Kenny looked down at the map. There were several areas highlighted in red, with the size of the circle indicating the affected area, all mostly similar to this odd lagoon here.

He shook his head, puzzled.

"I guess just keep following the map," he said. He started the motor, turning back out of the lagoon.

Then his phone beeped an alert in his pocket.

A text from Wyatt.

"*Drop what you're doing. Head for the Boneyard.*"

Then a second message.

"*The water-taxi just went down.*"

CHAPTER 25

By the time the water-taxi arrived at the Pike-house, they had only just discovered Adrienne and Dana missing, with both Josh and Paul.

At breakfast, Dave broke the news that the camp was closing to the group.

Amy and Anne drooped over their coffee. Henry shook his head sadly at Pamela, who nodded to Lori's own empty seat at the table.

Lori deliberately slept late, avoiding Dave's morning announcement, or else she might have realized then that Adrienne and Dana never came back.

Amy mentioned in passing that the group of them had been drinking and talked about going up to the hot-springs, but no one checked their rooms for at least an hour, and a search of the house turned-up nothing.

Lori woke to a knock at her door. She answered to find Dave looking grim.

"I've already reported them missing," he said. "And I'm told that's not even official for twenty-four hours. I don't know what else to do. We're all already leaving. If they got lost up in the hills, they would need a search party."

Dave looked over his shoulder as everyone behind him was already packed. The water-taxi would be there within the hour.

"I will inform your father's lawyers," he said.

Lori shut her eyes. If she never heard those words again in her life, that would be enough – even Dave still called them her father's lawyers.

Maybe it was best to be shut of these people – finally out on her own, square one. There were worse places to start.

"I assume you're staying?" Dave asked.

Lori nodded.

Dave looked at her sympathetically.

"Would you like me to stay? For just the next couple days?"

He stopped as the look on her face almost caused him to laugh.

"I'll take that as a *no*," he said. He reached into his pocket and handed her his card.

"Here's my contact information," he said. "I'll try and keep in front of this for you. But I think my firm may be separating our affairs if they end up liquidizing your remaining assets."

He sighed.

"I'm sorry," he said. "You can call me. I'll help you, where I can."

He sounded genuine. His tone touched a chord, and for a moment, Lori felt tears threaten – even a brief impulse to hug him. Pride kept that impulse safely at bay.

Outside, the water-taxi had just arrived at the dock, and the others were already lining up to board. Lori saw Norman at the wheel. Robbie was absent today.

There was also what looked like a party of three fishermen already onboard, presumably other refugees being escorted off the lake.

Pamela and Henry both hugged Lori goodbye.

"You keep your chin up," Pamela said. "You call if you ever need anything."

Dave was last onboard.

"If Adrienne and the others happen to show up, we'll send the boat back," he told Lori as she saw them off.

"I'm leaving you to handle things from here," he said. "You're a big girl, now. Wyatt will probably be in contact with you. He said a search party might still be hours away, but asked if you could keep yourself available."

"I could go check the hot-springs myself," Lori said. "At least we know that's where they were headed."

Dave shook his head.

"Wyatt doesn't want anyone going off by themselves just now. He said to just sit tight."

Lori shrugged apathetically.

"I'll keep my phone on," she said.

Dave paused, as if waiting for more. Then he simply nodded and turned to board the boat.

"Good luck," he said.

Lori stood on the dock until the boat pulled away. Pamela waved from the railing.

The water-taxi turned out of the cove into the main lake. Lori watched until they rounded the bend out of sight.

Then she turned back to her house – which, for now, was still *her* house – and realized she was about to finally be alone for the first time in her life. Maybe the only human being for miles.

Except for Sarah across the river, of course – who she still hadn't called.

And while she might be hosting first-responders of some kind if they ended-up needing a search party later, for now, the solitude was actually kind of nice.

Lori sat her phone down on the coffee-table, and lay down on her sofa. It was still only morning, but she was already burnt-out.

Without meaning to, she dozed. When she blinked awake, it was more than two hours later.

Rubbing her eyes, she checked her phone – still no messages.

She rose from the couch, looking out the window towards the hot-springs – an easy hike. She debated calling Wyatt, herself.

Instead, she simply went and put on her hiking-gear.

She had nothing else to do. She might as well go see.

In ten minutes, she was making her way up the slope.

CHAPTER 26

What happened was simple enough. Norman's eyesight wasn't what it was, so he was being safe and taking the southern route past Devil's Island, avoiding the treacherous Purgatory Cove.

He had been cruising the old stern-wheeler along this route for weeks now, mornings and evenings, so it wasn't as if he hadn't been on the lake.

What *was* new, was the tree that had broken loose, the same one Sarah spotted the day she arrived – it had drifted out of the Boneyard out into the middle of the lake.

It was a large tree, and would have been visible anywhere except right where it had settled in the deep water – directly along the center of the route Norman chose out of an excess of caution.

He might have spotted the log anyway, except his eyes had gone just a bit misty. It was a sour errand he was on today.

The kayakers he'd picked-up were wide-eyed after the pictures Wyatt showed them, and happy for the ride. But the party from the Pike-house was subdued.

Norman knew about the young man taken while skiing, but their head-count was down another two from the group he'd brought in yesterday.

Adrienne was one of the heads missing – Norm had liked her.

The administrator fellow, Dave, said they never came back after hiking up to the hot-springs.

They wouldn't be the first, Norman thought.

But for Norman, it might be the last. He'd been on the lake all his life, lived out his marriage, and entered his old-age here – he'd intended never to move.

Even with the lake closing, Norman knew he would likely keep his job if he wanted it – someone still had to perform basic duties – although, he suspected Robbie Ray's position might be cut from the budget.

Norman sighed. Maybe if *he* left, they might give the kid a break, and keep him on.

Still, the thought of leaving, after all this time, left him a little bit misty. It was like accepting a death – because the lake, itself, was terminal.

It brought a little sting to his eyes.

So, it might have been that, as much as old-age astigmatism, that caused him to miss the submerged tree, lurking barely four-feet below the surface, its roots tangled in the bottom, angled like a spear defending a castle.

That was the effect of it too.

The jagged trunk punctured and then tore the hull, as the boat continued to pass right over the surface, gouging-out the flat bottom, before spearing the spinning-propeller at the back like a golf-club impaling the rotor of a lawn mower.

The passengers were thrown forward in a mix of curses and screams.

Norman was knocked into his own wheel, smacking his face, stunning him long enough that he made no effort to stop the boat until momentum took them completely past the underwater tree, disemboweling their belly like a hooked-talon.

Almost immediately, the boat began to list. They were nearly half a mile from shore.

Norman blinked back to his senses as the motor died. He cranked the ignition and heard the grind of the broken wheel.

They were stuck. And sinking. They had minutes at best.

Norman pulled out his phone, bringing up Wyatt's number, one deliberate, laborious tap at a time.

In the back of the boat, screams erupted once again as water began to pour over the sides.

CHAPTER 27

Amy was first to realize the boat was going down, so she was the only one who wasn't almost immediately dumped into the lake. She was also a gymnast since second-grade, and almost without thinking, she literally vaulted over the top of Anne, Donna, *and* the three kayak-fishermen, up onto the roof of the cabin. Norman looked up as she thumped on the ceiling over his head.

The rest of the hapless passengers reacted a split-second later, almost in unison – screams mixed with shouts and curses, as the lake came rushing in, and they all knew full-well what might be coming in with it.

Henry and Pamela scrambled up after Amy, on top of the cabin, but the sinking boat abruptly tilted and they both toppled overboard.

The first of the kayakers swore unintelligibly, lunging for his inflatable boat, but the railing already dipped under the surface and dunked all three of them over the side.

Dave grabbed for the life-jackets, which Amy imagined was the least of their problems.

Air-pressure kept the cabin afloat, with Amy perched on top and Norman inside – the boat hung at the surface, bobbing like a giant fish-lure.

The rest of them were now swimming in open water.

A barrage of screams erupted. There was splashing and confusion.

After several moments, the screaming settled into whimpering.

But so far, there was nothing else.

"Hey," Dave said, treading water, looking around at the others, "I think we might be okay."

He moved towards one of the floating kayaks.

Then he was hit in the gut hard enough to make him grunt. He swallowed water, and started to choke, before something hit him again, like a fast-pitch in the thigh.

Then there was a fusillade of blows from all directions.

Watching not ten feet away, Anne screamed, as she saw the clouding blood. Donna began to cry.

Dave gurgled, struggling – fins and tails flapped in the fountaining-red water as the fish broke the surface.

Then the rest of the shoal came swarming in.

Amy wasn't sure who screamed first – it was impossible to tell if it was a man or a woman.

From her vantage atop the cabin, she could see a moving shadow materialize under the surface, surrounding the boat like an amorphous cloud made of nothing but flesh and teeth.

Dave's struggles were mostly over. Amy could see his face – it looked like he was trying to talk, but the only thing coming out were guttural chokes.

Then his head lulled, and he became a corpse.

He started to sink, his body still kicking and jerking with repeated impact from below.

It had taken seconds.

Now the cloud engulfed the others.

It wasn't like being in the water with circling sharks, where one person might get hit and another wouldn't. This was insectile – like a killer swarm of ravenous locusts that left nothing in its path – a wave that ran over all of them at once.

One of the fishermen had his kayak in hand, and his mates were both floundering after their own – if they could have right-sided even one of them, it might have made a difference, except that it required precious seconds they simply did not have.

Amy found herself looking each of them in the eye as they all three got hit – gutted and hollowed-out, muscle and tendon stripped away from still-kicking limbs.

It was hard to tell at what point they were actually dead.

Mercifully, it was probably early on. Less than the sixty-seconds for a cow.

Not so mercifully, they looked like long seconds.

Donna tried to swim for it – just a panic-driven bolt for shore – but she didn't get twenty-yards before Amy saw her start to struggle, and then drop beneath the surface.

Anne made a lunge for the pilot-house. Amy reached out her hand, but it was not even close.

As Anne lurched out of the water, Amy could see she had already been savaged – her open ribs were visible under missing breasts – her hip and pelvis were bare to the bone.

Amy flinched involuntarily from the reaching hand – although, she was hopelessly out of reach, so it probably didn't matter anyway.

Anne dropped back into the clear water, now clouded in red.

Amy watched her sink – her eyes were already fading, even before the fish hit her in force – she was giving up – letting herself go.

One second, she was there, staring-up at Amy as if still seeing.

Seconds later, her face was picked apart and gone – instead of the drifting, dreamy, fading expression on a human face, what stared up out of the bloody water was a hollow-eyed skull.

Anne's body jerked and jitterbugged as the fish dug into the meat of her, and her body finally sank from view.

Amy clung helplessly to the top of the pilot-house.

Norman was trapped inside with the water-level now at his eyes. His pocket of air was shrinking as the boat finally began to sink.

"*Oh no...,*" Amy said, her voice cracking, and tears starting to fall, as she realized it was her turn now too.

There was a loud crack of glass below.

One of the fish had charged the cabin, hitting the window like a six-pound softball. With the weight of the water behind it, the glass caved in.

Amy could hear Norman's last cries before the pilot-house was flooded.

"*Oh, Lord, Ethel, here I come!*"

The fish came bulling their way in with the rushing water. Norman was already underwater, so Amy couldn't hear him scream. But there were lots of bubbles. And blood.

Now the roof beneath her began to slip beneath the surface.

Amy screamed – she screamed loud and long, begging to God, before she was dropped into the already-frothing water.

Her screams hit a crescendo.

Mercifully, it was over in seconds.

But they were long seconds.

CHAPTER 28

Sarah was following Robbie's GPS signal, until it blinked off ten minutes ago. Service was always sketchy out here. Now she sat idling – she was not venturing any further until she saw Wyatt.

She was not afraid of Robbie – not *really* – but the game warden's presence would help stifle any personal conversations she didn't want to have.

Despite Wyatt's insinuation, it was definitely *not* about leftover sparks – sometimes time wasn't enough to chill such flames but circumstances certainly did.

Sarah very much wanted Robbie Ray to simply be someone she knew for a few months, one summer, a dozen years ago – a teenage love-song – one with a car-wreck at the end.

In the time since, he'd lived rough, been in prison. It was possible he held some of that against her.

But Sarah was determined the past remain in the past, and she was not, as an adult woman, about to be imposed any obligation to a grown-man on the weight of a seventeen-year-old girl's infatuation.

Still, she would feel more comfortable asserting that stance if Wyatt were present during the totality of their interaction.

As if summoned like a genie, her phone beeped Wyatt's ringtone – she'd given him the grim notes from the *Good, the Bad, and the Ugly.*

When she answered, however, his toneless words were more chilling.

"We've got a bad situation," he said, in his dead-flat voice. "The water-taxi went down. Out by the Boneyard."

He allowed exactly two-seconds for Sarah to absorb the full-impact of the statement, before giving her the rest, in a quick, military-style update.

"I've already got a chopper on the way. I texted Mitchell. Told him to get over there. You need to turn around too. I'll meet you there."

"What about the bodies Robbie found?"

"I'll call Robbie," Wyatt said. "Tell him to take pictures. And I guess he gets to take them back to the morgue himself."

For the first time, Sarah heard a hitch in his voice.

"I... think we're about to see a lot more."

There was a heartbeat of silence.

Sarah could envision it well enough – she knew what to expect.

"Who was on board?" she asked.

"I don't know yet," Wyatt replied. "I got a call from Norm. Went right to my voicemail. Said they were going down in the Boneyard. That was twenty minutes ago. Goddamned service out here. I tried to call back, and he isn't responding. That councilor-fellow isn't answering either."

Sarah shut her eyes. It wouldn't have mattered. Whatever happened would have been over long before anyone got there.

Sixty-seconds or less.

"You turn on around," Wyatt instructed. "I'll see you at the Boneyard."

Sarah glanced towards the cove where Robbie said he would be waiting.

"Okay," she said, "I'll see you there."

She hung up, turning the wheel.

As she did so, her phone rang again in her hand. She looked down and saw Robbie's Field and Game number.

A moment later, her phone alerted her to a text.

"You might as well answer. I'm right behind you."

Sarah turned and now saw Robbie's boat separating from the overgrown brush near shore. Frowning, she answered his call.

"Waiting in ambush?" she said.

"Kinda," Robbie replied. "I've been watching you. I turned off my phone so you couldn't GPS my exact location."

He was in waving-distance now, puttering his boat up alongside hers. He tapped off his phone, smiling mildly.

"I thought it was possible," he said, "if you spotted me here alone, you might just turn and leave."

He shrugged.

"Go figure."

"Wyatt just called," Sarah replied. "He says there's been an accident, and to turn around right away."

"So," Robbie said quickly, "he's not coming?"

Sarah blinked, wondering if she'd said too much.

Robbie chuckled wryly.

"I already heard you talking. Voices carry on the lake."

At that moment, Robbie's own phone rang. He retrieved it from his pocket, his smile dimming as he saw Wyatt's number.

"Yessir?" he answered, putting the call on speaker.

"We've got a situation," Wyatt, began, but Robbie interrupted.

"I know, Sarah's already here."

Wyatt paused.

"Everybody working and playing together?" he asked.

"I'm fine," Sarah called over.

"And I already took my video, Officer Wyatt," Robbie added, the picture of a model-inmate.

"Well, then," Wyatt replied, "I guess you've got some dead bodies to transport to town, Mr. Ray. And you can send the lady on her way. We've got dead people out this direction too."

Robbie glanced over at Sarah standing in her boat.

"You want me to show her what I found? Just so long as she's here?"

"I'm fine, if the lady's fine," Wyatt answered. "But I want her headed this way within the hour. Understood?"

"Is the lady fine?" Robbie asked, tipping the phone to Sarah.

She eyed him narrowly, but nodded.

"I won't be long, Wyatt," she said.

"I'll be checking in," he replied. The line beeped off.

Robbie shrugged expectantly.

"Well?" he said. "Want to see the first one?"

He turned his boat in the direction of the shore, tapping at his phone while he did so. Sarah's phone beeped and video began to play on her screen.

"I filmed each of them, as I found them," Robbie called over the motor.

He led them along the shallow cove, tucked unobtrusively off the main loch, like her own lagoon. And just the same, she saw floating patches of water-lilies, lined along the surface like sunlamps, perhaps warming the water just enough to trick the fish below, and induce them to breed.

Sarah reached over the side with her boat-hook, plucking one of the floating lilies off the surface, and sure enough, the dead, discolored eggs were there, like jelly gone hard in a refrigerator

Again, that *could* be a positive – these fish were acclimated, but still constrained by the base physiology of their species. They were normal fish – nothing genetically-altered. With Leo Pike, Sarah would have expected nothing less.

On the other hand, it *was* a very *healthy* population, that managed without Leo Pike's care for over a decade. And while there must be others, the one viable nest that she'd found was survivable, but hardly optimum.

She ran her finger self-consciously over the lump of bandage under her jeans – a divot taken out of her hip like she might have bitten out of an apple.

The fish she'd encountered on this lake were *optimum*.

Then her ears perked.

"Wait," she said. "Did you hear that?"

Sarah shut off her motor, motioning for Robbie to do the same.

After a moment, the sound came again.

Not a dozen yards away, the lake surface bubbled-up a *big* bullfrog-belch. Sarah saw a swell in the water nearly five-feet across, followed by steady, popping puffs of steam burped into the mountain air.

She dipped her hand briefly into the water. Right here at this spot, was warm. Two-hundred yards further out, it was cold as ever.

"There's a vent right here," Sarah said.

It was, in fact, a *large* vent – this cove was getting a good deal of geothermal mix. If this was the case all over the lake, Sarah would be surprised if all this seismic activity hadn't left the underground vent-shafts and tunnels honeycombed and flooded beneath the lake floor – interconnected, like a thermally-heated hamster-runway for fish.

She looked around the cove.

"You found the first body right near here?"

Robbie pointed to the trees lining the shore, many of them trunk-deep in the lake, similar to the Boneyard. Sarah could see a larva-white mass floating, tangled in the branches.

Sarah didn't need a closer look to know what it was. Something – a sense of responsibility, perhaps? – forced her to, anyway.

She steered behind Robbie as he puttered up beside the body, deftly reaching down with his gaff, hauling the picked-clean skeleton aboard.

These remains had been out a lot longer than those she'd seen at the morgue – mostly bones. And leftover hiking-gear.

Sarah sent Wyatt a quick text.

"*I think you can account for at least five of your missing-hikers.*"

And then:

"*When people go hiking around here, it's usually up to the hot-springs.*"

After a moment, Wyatt sent back an *okay*-sign.

Robbie led her to the next body, following a path leading directly from the vent. The second was in the same condition as the first.

But it wasn't just human corpses floating around them.

Robbie stood in his boat, pointing.

"Look there."

Bundled unobtrusively under a branch was a gnarled tangle of fur, horns, and bones – all gnawed, skeletonized remains, packed together as if regurgitated from the bowels of some massive giant.

They looked cooked.

"These animals didn't die here," Sarah said. "They were kicked out by the vent. And they've been exposed to heat."

Sarah looked north to where the funnel of the Cauldron channeled the misty steam from the hot-springs.

The entire area was bursting with geologic-pressure, but the springs were the obvious suspect.

"I think I've seen enough," Sarah said, as Robbie pulled the third body onboard, this one with strips of long-hair still attached – another woman.

"Sarah, wait..." Robbie said, turning quickly, almost dropping the corpse.

She paused, looking back warily.

He eyed her seriously.

"We *are* going to have a talk," he told her. "You and I. Sooner or later. You *owe* me that, Sarah."

"Well," she replied cautiously, "maybe I do, or maybe I don't. But right now, we're both on the clock."

Robbie nodded.

"Fair enough," he said, reaching back over the side, pulling the long-haired cadaver back onboard. "Help me load the bodies?"

Sarah shook her head, cranking her motor back up.

"I don't think so," she said.

Robbie smiled sardonically, dropping the dead woman on the floor.

Sarah had just started to turn away when something caught her eye, registering significance.

"Wait," she said, turning back. "Let me see."

Robbie held the body back up. It was still attached to ropes and a harness.

Not just hiking-gear – *climbing* gear.

And there was only one place on the lake where you needed climbing gear.

The Cauldron.

CHAPTER 29

Sarah noted the heavier-than-normal smokestack emanating from the Cauldron's peak as she approached Devil's Island.

To the south, waited the scene at the Boneyard. She had already gotten texts from Deb and Kenny: "*We just arrived – first on the scene – it looks bad.*"

And a few minutes later: "*Very VERY bad.*"

They sent her a picture of the sunken boat, with barely six-inches of the cabin-roof still visible above the surface.

Shortly after, Sarah saw an emergency chopper fly past overhead.

How many people were on that boat? Half-a-dozen? More?

Sarah had already seen several bodies today, decayed and rotting over long weeks. By the time she reached the Boneyard, victims of today's accident would have been recovered.

These would be fresh.

She paused, looking after the chopper – not a rescue, she thought grimly, a clean-up.

But Sarah thought she understood how it all happened now.

She'd suspected something like it all along, turning her eyes to the Cauldron.

Usually, the smoke-like emanations would dwindle during the day – except for the hot-springs, themselves, most of the mist disappeared from the lake.

But as Sarah took a measured look, it appeared vapor was rising from the Cauldron itself.

She recalled the time she'd fallen in – how ice-cold that water had been.

Sarah pulled out her phone, tapping up her temperature records. They were slightly higher in the area, but not significantly – not even as high as her own cove.

Of course, her color-coded map didn't show underground thermal-heat, which was all over.

Sarah eyed the not-too-distant peak of the Cauldron.

On impulse, she veered left, north of Devil's Island into Purgatory Cove.

Deb and Kenny were sufficient scholarly authority on-site at the wreck.

And truth to tell, Sarah wasn't quite ready to see it until she knew who had gone down with the ship.

She didn't *think* Lori would have vacated her own house with the others. And the other passengers were basically strangers.

Well... except for old Norman.

Maybe she was being cowardly, unwilling to face another face-full of gore.

On the other hand, she genuinely believed she was on to something.

Keeping a safe distance from the tricky north shore, Sarah made her route through the deeper, not-quite-so-treacherous water running nearer the island.

The wind was picking-up. Sarah could hear the Cauldron whistling right along with it. Up ahead, the broken, extended peak loomed like a totem.

Cautiously, Sarah turned into the shallow water. The cave/tunnel to the basin was blocked off, but there was a narrow, rocky beach, and you could hike up the hill to the top.

Fish and Game maintained a small dock back when the Cauldron was still a recreational area – the remaining relic had fallen into disrepair, wobbling uncertainly when Sarah tied a mooring rope, and a little more as she climbed the ladder.

The Cauldron towered a hundred-feet of sheer cliff from the beach. Sarah looked up at the steady stream of vapor pouring out the top. She pulled out her phone and sent a text to Wyatt.

"I think the Cauldron might be a hot-spot."

She was about to add to that message when her phone beeped in her hand. She tapped the screen, expecting to see a response from Wyatt.

Instead, it was Robbie's number again.

"You gonna climb that?" it said.

And then her phone rang.

Another text beeped.

"You might as well pick up. I'm right behind you."

Sarah turned around to see his boat trailing fifty yards in her wake.

"Again," she said. "Sneaking around a lot, these days."

Although, he *had* been known to do that in the past – like how he appeared at the Pike-place that night.

That hadn't worked out so well.

Sarah clicked-off her phone and waited for him to motor-up to the dock. He smiled disarmingly, with five cannibalized bodies piled on the deck at his feet.

"So," he said. "You going to climb that thing? I got gear."

"Robbie," Sarah said patiently, "Wyatt told you to take those bodies into town."

Robbie nodded.

"I am. I'm just taking the long way."

Sarah's phone beeped again in her hand – Wyatt responding with a *thumbs-up* to her text.

"That's Wyatt," she said. "I could call him right now."

Robbie nodded archly, tying off his boat, grabbing up an armful of gear, and climbing up on the wobbly dock beside her.

"You do that," he said. "See if you can send me to prison."

He gave her an up-and-down frown, as he pushed by her, heading up the hill.

"Me, I'm gonna see what's in there."

Sarah glared after him.

He paused, looking back.

"Sarah," he said, "be a courageous person. What exactly do you think I'm going to do?"

"Well," she said, "you've been creeping around. What do stalker-types *usually* do?"

"You wouldn't give me access to you."

"That's up to *me*," she returned hotly. "*Not* you."

Robbie stared back. Sarah thought she'd sparked his temper. But then he shrugged.

"You come if you want," he said, as he hiked his pack, turned, and headed uphill.

Sarah stared after him, eyes narrowed.

After a moment, she followed.

It was a short hike up to the Cauldron's peak, fairly steep as you circled back through the woods, but doable in street shoes – still, Sarah found herself sweating.

Humidity was constant on Lake Perdition. It made things generally uncomfortable, particularly this time of year – first you got sweaty, then that mountain wind would whip through, leaving you chilled and shivering.

Today, it was warmer on the hill.

The steam venting through the vents from the not-far-distant hot-springs was always thin, and usually cooled by the mountain air.

Sarah held up her hand to the drifting vapor, as she neared the peak.

This was warm – almost sultry.

Robbie was waiting at the edge as Sarah walked up beside him, looking down into the basin. The foliage lining the sides was cloaked in mist like a miniature rain-forest.

Sarah started to lean forward when the rock beneath her feet cracked.

She let out a brief shriek, but Robbie had already snatched her arm and pulled her back.

Three-feet of the ledge simply crumbled away – there was the echoing clatter of impact as the loose rubble hit both rock and water, a hundred-feet below.

Sarah looked around the inner lip of the Cauldron. The constant heat, cold, and freezing water-vapor, was turning all this dried-up lava-rock brittle.

"Over here," Robbie said, pulling her cautiously back towards the trees, where the thick roots clung more firmly to the earth.

He picked a larger tree and wrapped his rope around the trunk, attaching his climbing harness around his waist. He tossed the second rope at Sarah's feet.

"I'll go by myself," he said, smiling. "If you're afraid."

Sarah glared. She was ashamed to admit it, but that was actually the line that had worked on her the first time.

But this wasn't a ride on the back of a Harley.

Robbie hooked his harness, and looked over at her expectantly.

"Well? Are you coming?"

Sarah looked cautiously over the edge. She'd done this climb many times – she grew-up crawling over every hill within hiking distance.

Although it *had* been a few years since she'd climbed anything.

Knowing full-well she was probably being foolish, she grabbed the rope, tied-off to her own tree, and snapped the harness around her waist.

She shrugged. Robbie smiled.

"Okay, let's go,"

With that, he dropped back off the edge.

Her heart beating, Sarah looked down – a hundred feet – she would have been on the basin floor in sixty-seconds back in the old days.

Taking a breath, trying to move smoothly and calmly, just like going down stairs. Her rope rubbed against the cliff wall as she stepped over, kicking loose more rocks.

"Hey!" Robbie objected from below. "Be careful!"

Sarah shut her eyes, squeezing her ascender-latch, suddenly releasing the catch. She dropped a heart-stopping ten-feet before she remembered to pinch the lever shut again.

Robbie paused, hanging twenty-feet beneath her.

"You okay up there?"

Sarah took an irritated breath.

"Yes," she said crossly, looking back over her shoulder. "I'm fine, thank you."

She put her feet against the cliff-wall, and began to drop down.

As she did so, her rope knocked more rocks loose, and a baseball-sized chunk dropped, bouncing right off her head.

There was a bolt of pain and a bright light. For a moment, Sarah went limp and her hand simply relaxed on the lever – she dropped nearly ten feet, before snapping back to soupy semi-consciousness, clenching the brake, jerking to a stop.

But she was dazed, and it took all her focus to keep her hand squeezed tight.

Then she felt Robbie's arm around her as he swung over to catch her, running his feet along the cliff-wall.

Still not quite coherent, Sarah turned to grab hold of him, inadvertently letting go of her rope. Catching her weight over one arm, Robbie felt his own rope starting to pull loose.

"Awww *shit*," he muttered, as he released the latch on his harness, kicking down the wall like a commando, scraping down more rocks.

They were still thirty-feet up when he felt his rope slip its knot loose from the tree.

Below was water. Or the rocky embankment.

Call it.

Robbie pushed with both feet off the cliff wall, Sarah on one shoulder, throwing her towards the edge.

Semi-conscious, she hit the rocks awkwardly, landing hard – she screamed as her leg broke just below the knee. The sudden pain jerked her fully-awake, even as she tumbled into the basin wall.

Robbie didn't quite make the ledge – he hit the pond dead center.

The first thing he thought was that it was warm.

Next, he wondered if he was about to die.

He plunged deep beneath the clear surface – covered like a tarp with lily pads – before he jackknifed underwater and immediately began kicking for the ledge.

Seconds ticked – a cow only needed sixty – but nothing touched him yet.

Then something nipped his arm. Then the leg.

Robbie realized what happened – the rocks had dropped from above, and probably did so all the time – piranha were fish, and would scatter.

At first.

Now they were back on him.

He felt three more hits before launching himself up onto the rocks, beside where Sarah was sprawled, holding her broken leg.

Robbie looked down at five different holes bitten out of him, cup-shaped and bleeding. The largest, on his arm, was the size of a quarter.

"Juveniles," Sarah said, "count yourself lucky."

She looked around at the pond and a mini-ecosystem that had no business being there.

"It's a nursery," she said.

CHAPTER 30

Wyatt sat back and let the official machinery do its work.

The Search and Rescue team loaded the bodies aboard their chopper.

A state policeman oversaw the recovery, a by-the-book trooper named Jacobs, who Wyatt had worked with before. Today, he referred Officer Jacobs to Kenny and Deb, who were first on the scene, besides being the two science brains.

Wyatt watched as the chopper-crew fished out each body, using hooks, treating the water as if it was acid.

The clear surface revealed nothing. Wyatt didn't know whether the fish were hiding in the rocks, or had simply left the area, but the whole Boneyard seemed empty, as if the fish had fled the scene of the crime.

They hadn't – as one of the chopper-crew discovered after he pulled what looked like the remains of one of the councilor-girls up beside the helicopter's pontoons, and there was a sudden rush from below.

The fleshless corpse itself seemed to struggle on the end of his hook – the crewman jerked back, dropping both back in the water.

"Jesus," he said, wide-eyed. "Did you *see* that?"

The water roiled briefly below, and then stilled. Wyatt could see fat, torpedo-like bodies darting off. They had responded to movement but there wasn't enough meat left to keep them interested.

Cautiously, the crewman snatched his hook back, and grabbed hold of the dead girl.

Wyatt recognized her hair. She had been a pretty one. So was her friend. Not so pretty anymore.

They pulled old Norman out next.

It was harder to tell with the next few – could be the kayakers, or maybe that camp-director fellow.

Wyatt hung on his name a moment. *Dave.*

Somewhere in the collection of skeletonized corpses, were Henry and Pamela.

Officer Jacobs had Kenny and Deb examine each body as they were fished out, methodically jotting down every question, and filming everything with his phone.

Kenny did most of the talking, as Deb seemed to be fighting dry-heaves.

Once the bodies were loaded, Jacobs turned to Wyatt.

"I'll put out a spot on the news," he said. "I got enough video to run. Hopefully, that'll help keep folks off the lake."

"Or attract a bunch of nuts," Wyatt replied.

Jacobs shrugged.

"Well, at least, maybe they'll be informed nuts who ought to have known better."

Wyatt nodded, as Jacobs stepped under spinning rotors and boarded the chopper. Wyatt held his hat from the wind-blast as the copter lifted into the air, then turned towards town.

The sunken wreck of the water-taxi looked to stay where it was, as Wyatt could think of no practical way for a crew to pull it out. As if it were even a priority.

But now that the human clean-up was done, Wyatt's eyes turned to Deb and Kenny, and realized someone was missing.

The same thought occurred simultaneously to Kenny.

"Wasn't Sarah supposed to be on her way?" he asked.

Wyatt glanced at his watch.

Yes, she was. Two hours ago.

He tapped her number. After nine rings it went to voicemail. Then he tried Robbie, who on last-check, had been right there with her.

No answer there, either.

Wyatt crooked a worried eye at the other two.

"That might not be good," he said.

Deb tried her own phone, calling the same number, and got the same voicemail.

Wyatt checked his messages. The last texts from Sarah were about the hot-springs. And then the Cauldron. He turned to the others.

"Would she have just taken it upon herself to go up there alone?"

Kenny and Deb exchanged glances, before both nodded affirmatively.

"Okay, then," Wyatt said, "you two take the Cauldron. I'll check the hot-springs."

CHAPTER 31

As she hiked up the trail to the hot-springs, Lori found herself remembering the litter.

People were always so *good* about cleaning-up their own waste – the type prone to hoof-it miles into the woods just to soak in natural springs tended to carry a certain respect for nature. Lori had found it disheartening to see rubbish left behind.

But people picked up their trash *after* they bathed.

What if they just never came out?

Yesterday, the hot-springs were as still and idyllic as ever, and she had seen nothing suspicious in its clear waters.

She had almost climbed in herself.

Today, the clearing looked no different – quiet and undisturbed.

Except for the pile of clothes lying unobtrusively on the bank.

That was always one of the selling points for the college kids – no clothes allowed in the hot-springs. Like the Playboy mansion's 'Grotto'.

Lori stood a moment, absorbing the significance of that small pile – two bikini-tops, two pairs of shorts, along with a couple pairs of denim jeans and flannel shirts. And towels.

The hot-springs bubbled with thermal pressure from below, and Lori began walking along the bank, peering into the water.

Further out, where the lilies had grown thick, the floating leaves seemed to ripple, as if with a strong wind.

In fact, it almost seemed like a whirlpool-effect, drawing circling debris like a filter in a pool.

And just along the bank, she now saw a tangled mass caught in the brush.

As Lori moved closer, she realized a woman's arm was reaching out of the water, her hand still clinging to the branches. Her hair identified her as Adrienne.

Lori reached over with a loose branch. There were clearly no signs of life, but what she could see still had skin. Adrienne's unmarked face, pale and dead, lulled over the branches she clung to – perhaps trying to pull herself out.

Could she and the others have simply drowned? Every year, people died in normal hot-tubs – they just overheated and passed-out.

She prodded the half-floating body with a stick, and it rolled in the water.

Now Lori could see everything *below* the neck and right arm was eaten to the bone.

Not a drowning.

Adrienne's dead, clinging hand pulled free of the branch. There was a splash as the rest of her dropped into the water.

A frenzy of movement exploded beneath the surface, flashing fins and teeth, almost too fast to see, tearing into the clinging morsels that remained.

Lori jerked back quickly. Adrienne's body struggled and jerked at the surface, as if she were dying all over again.

The fish were small – six-inches or less. Youngsters.

Adrienne was pulled below. Lori could see them swarming over the last bits of her – the dead, vacant-stare was soon gone as they consumed what was left of her face.

Lori's stomach roiled, and she turned away.

Her foot slipped in the mud.

She pitched forward, a four-foot drop into the water – she was going in face-first, right into the frenzy below.

But then, even as her face splashed into the water, and she saw the first incoming snap of teeth, she was snatched by the back of her shorts and yanked back up onto the bank.

Lori stood blinking at Wyatt, with his hand latched on the back of her trousers like a mama cat carrying a kitten.

Wyatt – always showing up suddenly.

He held on firmly until Lori got her footing, and stepped back from the bank.

"I came up the back way from the rapids," he said. "I found the others. Looks like both Mullins boys and the other councilor girl."

Wyatt nodded to the far side of the springs.

"There are at least a couple more vents like this breaking through," he said. "I think it's spitting this spring-water right out into the lake. Your friend Sarah was right. All these vents are interconnected underground."

He eyed Lori meaningfully.

"I came up looking for *her*, by the way," he said. "Sarah is currently missing." He nodded back at the remains of Adrienne. "At this point, I'm happy we haven't found her."

He tapped his phone, sending a text to Kenny.

"She's not here. But we can write-off our missing councilors."

A message came back from Deb's number.

"We're at the Cauldron. They're here. We need help."

Wyatt nodded, typing back.

"*I'm on my way.*"

He pocketed his phone, turning back to Lori.

"Looks like they've found her," he said.

Lori looked back where Adrienne's body still twitched, just below the surface.

"What about *her*?"

"She and the others are dead. Not a priority. But if we hurry, maybe we can catch somebody still alive." He checked his watch. "It hasn't happened *yet*, today, but it's still early."

Wyatt turned on his heel, heading down the path towards the Cauldron.

Lori saw the steam rising over the trees – smoking brimstone from the netherworlds below. Modern men called it geothermal-heat, but it still fit the description of Hell.

She glanced back in the hot-springs pool, where the water around Adrienne had finally stilled.

Lori's face was still wet, from where she'd nearly fallen in, herself. She shivered, a delayed reaction, as she realized how close it had really been.

She turned and followed Wyatt down the hill.

CHAPTER 32

That was how they *all* fell, Sarah thought, looking up at the crumbling ledge.

She winced, tears squirting from her eyes, as Robbie tended to her leg.

The Cauldron walls effectively blocked cell-signals, so any rescue was likely hours away, and Sarah was again forced to submit to near-unwilling first-aid, as Robbie clumsily attempted to splint her cracked shin with a few sticks and strips of his shirt.

Robbie was not so light a touch as Wyatt, and it turned out a broken-leg hurt a *lot* more than the piranha-bites on her ass.

Sarah deliberately occupied her mind with a scientific examination of the habitat that bloomed around them.

Most of it was explained by the steady belch of the vent – a *big* ol' bullfrog this time – that seemed to have broken open nearly the entire floor of the Cauldron's basin.

The combination of heated steam from below, with often-freezing temperatures above, left the ledge a crumbling pit-fall. That accounted for both the hikers and the moose – they fell in, and the vent flushed them out into the middle of the lake.

Mystery solved. A freak ecological event. Sarah hoped she lived to write about it.

She wiped running sweat from her eyes. It was like a sauna in the basin. With the packed lilies and congested vegetation in a protected space, you couldn't have asked for a more optimum breeding-ground on the Amazon itself.

Piranha had been reproducing on the lake for years, unmolested and unseen as they traveled the thermal-heated runways – eating the hatchery's trout, bringing down plant-efficiency enough so they couldn't buck the pressure to close – in turn, cutting off the food.

It took longer to pare-down those invasive catfish.

But now, they had all those optimum breeding conditions, with a robust, healthy, and physically *large* population, that was now starving.

It was a simple equation – cut down the protein, but maintain the same calorie-requirements, you get more-than-normal aggression.

Robbie's thumb squeezed her cracked shinbone as he tied off the last strap. Sarah grunted, wiping one last squirt of a tear off her cheek.

"Sorry," Robbie said, sitting back to examine his own bites, which he also attempted to patch with tatters of his shirt – blood continued to run freely, leaving his arms and torso zebra-striped in red.

He looked out at the surrounding sequestered pond and sighed.

"This all came from *that* night, didn't it?"

Sarah eyed him cautiously.

"In a butterfly-effect-dropped-into-a-perfect-storm sort of way, perhaps."

She offered nothing more. Trapped, injured and bleeding, she could handle. But Robbie had her at his mercy now. She watched to see if he would take advantage.

Predictably, he did.

"You know, it would be easy to be angry with you," he said. "You just blew town forever. What's it been? Twelve years? You never even talked to me again."

He frowned.

"I just got out of jail, by the way. That was where you left me, remember?"

"You were never charged with anything because of *me* or because of that night," Sarah answered quickly. "You became a convict all on your own."

He smiled bitterly. "Yeah. I got there anyway. The town saw to it. And *that* was over that night, for sure. And you just left me to swing."

"I told police I didn't remember what happened."

It was true – she *had* told them that, and at the time, she didn't.

Robbie would not know her alcohol-induced amnesia wore off. Sarah saw no reason to put it on the record.

"Yeah," he said, bitterly. "You certainly were not a drinker." He nodded affirmatively. "But *I* was. It's ironic. I was the only one who actually lied to the police about that night. Because *I* remembered *everything*."

His eyes faded for a moment, far away, as if seeing it all again.

"You know," he said, "sometimes, I think everything that's happened to me was because of what you and I did together. Karma-punishment."

But he shook his head.

"Except nothing ever happened to *you*."

Sarah didn't like the sound of that.

She had always assumed his booze-recall of that night would have been much better than the rest of them. That did not make it a memory she wanted to share. She remembered it all just fine, thank you, and felt no need to be confronted with anything.

"I still have the video of us," Robbie said. "The one Danielle found on my phone. That was how she found out about us."

Sarah's frown darkened.

Well, there it was.

She knew that video, alright. It was footage of their second night together, and Sarah had been at *least* as scandalized as Danielle, when she found Robbie had taken it. She still remembered him promising to erase it.

Yet, it still existed to this day.

"It's a good thing," Robbie said, "Danielle's death was ruled an accident, or the cops might have kept looking, and probably found it. I'm sure you wouldn't have wanted *that* to go public."

He shrugged.

"Maybe that's something to consider, the next time your friend Hayden Marshall Wyatt brings up my probation officer."

Sarah's eyes narrowed. Was he really going this low? Blackmailing her with a teenage sex-tape?

It seemed very non-desperado. More creepy than bad-boy.

They traded stares, each measuring the other.

Then there was a sudden clatter of rubble bouncing down off the Cauldron walls. The falling rock was followed by Kenny's voice.

"Hey! Are you guys down there?"

Robbie nodded to Sarah.

"We'll talk later," he said. Then he turned and shouted up. "We're down here! And watch those rocks. The whole area is brittle as shale."

There was the sound of more cracking rock and tumbling rubble, followed by Kenny, "*Jesus.*"

"Are either of you hurt?" Deb shouted.

"Sarah's got a busted shin," Robbie hollered back. "She can't climb. You need to call a chopper."

"Terrific," Kenny said. "We just sent our chopper back with a bunch of dead bodies. It's probably unloading, refueling. Maybe on its way back to Lewiston. Probably an hour before it gets here."

"Here," Deb said, tapping at her phone. "I'm texting Wyatt."

After a moment, she looked up. "He's on his way."

Kenny peeked down over the drop-off.

"If we got a rope down to you, could we pull Sarah up?"

"You're not pulling anything," Sarah hollered back. "Seriously, Kenny. You two can't pull us up. Just wait for a chopper."

Kenny looked down, indecisive.

"At least wait for Wyatt," Deb said.

"Fine," Kenny said, stepping back from the edge. "Let's try and get the chopper coming."

He tapped his phone.

But then there was a loud crack as the rock beneath his feet collapsed.

Sarah saw the crust of the ledge fall away, just as it surely had for the moose and all those hikers.

Kenny let out a shriek as he fell with it. Deb screamed, reaching out a desperate hand, missing widely, and probably luckily, or he would have dragged her with him over the edge.

Robbie groaned, shaking his head. Sarah could hardly bear to watch.

Kenny briefly caught hold of the ledge, but that piece broke off in his hand.

It also might have saved his life because the effort swung him against the wall into the creeper vegetation that grew there.

A man once tried to scale those creepers, Sarah remembered. The foliage broke away. He had fallen and died.

But he made it *part* of the way.

Kenny clung to the roots and branches, seventy-feet up, panting, maybe with his eyes shut.

Deb's head poked over the edge.

"Oh my God, Kenny, are you alive?"

"I'm here," he shouted back, although he didn't sound confident.

"You have to climb!" Sarah shouted up. "It's only thirty-feet. You can make it. Just be careful your handholds can hold your weight."

"Yeah, and what am I supposed to do if they can't?" Kenny shouted back.

But he began to climb.

"Come on," Deb urged, almost whispering, "you can make it."

Smaller rocks were already breaking loose, undermining the roots. With ten-feet to go, Kenny felt a sudden rip as one branch tore completely free of the wall, sending loose soil and brittle lava down into the basin. There was splashing as they hit the water.

Kenny caught hold of a thicker branch.

"Oh my God, Kenny," Deb said. "If you live, I'm going to kill you."

Gasping, he climbed the last few feet to the ledge. He reached up and grabbed Deb's outstretched hand.

For just a moment, they hung there.

"Oh what the hell," Kenny said. "Will you marry me?"

Deb barked a chirp of cautionary laughter.

"Oh, you *better* have already bought a ring," she said.

Then the rock ledge collapsed beneath both of them.

This time, the entire four-foot section broke away, separating from the wall, and they both tumbled amidst the debris, into the reservoir pond.

There was a brief scream from Deb as they dropped away from the wall, but both of them were battered by several hundred-pounds of rock – probably a kindness as they fell into the water unconscious.

The rocks hit the water, drenching both Sarah and Robbie on their ledge.

Underwater, the piranha scattered.

Deb and Kenny both bobbed to the surface, floating face-down. It was impossible to tell if they were alive. But in another moment, it didn't matter, because the fish came swarming back.

Neither Kenny nor Deb responded as their bodies were violently tugged and jerked from below.

It was a typically short affair. Kenny rolled in the water, and Sarah could see his eyes already eaten out, and most of his face was gone, leaving just his teeth and hair.

Deb was pulled below.

Sarah and Robbie sat silently on their ledge.

"He fell," Robbie remarked, unhappily, "*before* he called for the chopper."

Sarah nodded. That left Wyatt. And nothing to do but wait.

She stared steadfastly at the water, determined not to speak. For the moment, Robbie respected her silence – she had just watched two of her oldest friends die.

Sarah shut her eyes, wondering if she was in shock, for she felt no urge to cry.

Out in the pond, Deb's corpse bobbed to the surface, tatters of clothes and strips of hair still clinging to the stripped bone.

Sarah checked her watch.

Sixty-seconds or less.

CHAPTER 33

Lori panted as she tried to keep up with Wyatt through the woods. She had no idea how old he was, maybe twice her age, but he loped along ahead of her, light-footed as an Indian, and never even seemed to break above a walk, while Lori was having trouble keeping up with him at a half-jog.

It was a mile to the Cauldron, over rugged terrain. By the time their path finally broke through the trees, Lori was winded and drenched in sweat.

Wyatt was already standing at the ledge, peering over – his hand was latched onto the branch of one of the trees lining the Cauldron's north upper-lip.

Lori jogged up beside him, panting.

Almost immediately, the rocky ledge beneath her feet began to crack.

Lori's heart skipped a beat – she backpedaled but Wyatt's adder-fast hands had already snatched her back beside him under the tree. He pointed down to where the roots held a solid grip into the earth.

"For God's sake," a man's voice hollered up out of the basin. "Stay away from the edge."

Robbie's voice.

"Is Sarah with you?" Wyatt hollered down.

"I'm here," Sarah called back.

"Where's Mitchell?"

There was a brief pause. When Sarah answered, her voice was deliberately toneless.

"They fell in," she said. "They're both gone."

Lori blinked. She'd known Kenny and Deb as long as she'd known Sarah.

In the time it took for them to hike a mile from the springs, they were both already gone.

Wyatt sighed.

"Well, it's already been a pretty bad, goddamned day," he muttered.

Then he leaned over the edge and shouted down.

"I called our chopper. They already landed in Lewiston. They're refueling and they won't be able to take off for at least thirty-minutes. Can you climb?"

"Sarah's got a busted shin," Robbie called back. "She can't climb."

"*I* can climb," Sarah interjected. "Just get me a harness. I'm not a damned paraplegic. I can use a ratchet, and I can bump up the wall with my other foot."

"It's up to you," Wyatt held up his rope. "The chopper's got a harness too."

"Get us out," Sarah said. "I want out of here now."

Wyatt turned and tied the rope to the trunk of the tree, motioning Lori to step back. He pulled the climbing gear from his pack and threaded the ropes through the harness.

Securing his footing on the tree roots, he tossed the rope down into the basin.

Robbie caught the rope at the bottom.

Helping Sarah to her one good foot, he strapped the harness around her, then hollered up to Wyatt and Lori.

"She's ready!"

He turned to Sarah.

"See you up there," he said.

And then, eyeing her meaningfully, "We'll talk soon."

Sarah's eyes narrowed, but she said nothing. Instead, she simply grabbed the rope, hopped her one good foot up on the wall, and cranked the ascender-lever, pulling herself up one measured foot at a time.

She got exactly twenty-feet before she stopped, dangling, one foot propped up against the rock.

"What's the matter?" Wyatt hollered down.

"I'm stuck," she called back. "The latch is frozen."

Sarah struggled with the lever, trying to use both hands, but her balance was hampered by her injured leg, and she bounced off the wall with her one good foot.

Finally, Robbie grabbed the bottom of the rope and began to climb up after her.

"Careful," Wyatt shouted down. "You just more than doubled the weight on that rope."

Robbie monkeyed-up just below Sarah, reaching for her harness as she dangled awkwardly above him.

"Where are you stuck...?" he began, before the ascender-latch suddenly came free – Sarah dropped an abrupt six-feet, before she managed to squeeze the lever shut again.

She landed on top of Robbie, knocking his grip loose from the rope.

Twisting in midair like a cat, Robbie grabbed hold of the creeping vines and branches draping the Cauldron wall, catching hold as Kenny had done.

Unfortunately, Robbie was heavier, and his handholds pulled away from the rock almost immediately. For one precarious moment, he dangled over the water.

Then he pushed off the wall with both feet, lunging for the dangling rope.

At the same moment, Sarah turned, reaching for his outstretched hand. Instead, she struck it, knocking him away, and Robbie missed his grip.

He dropped into the water, landing with a splash.

Robbie came up, sputtering.

Dangling above, Sarah could see the fish scatter, just like after the falling rocks. Robbie lurched into a full-out propeller stroke for the ledge.

But the fish recognized the difference.

Sarah saw them swarm upon him, smaller than the big adults out on the main lake, but there were a lot of them – congested.

Robbie screamed.

Sarah watched as Robbie was eaten in brutal, time-lapse stop-motion.

Then the water clouded with blood, churning in a swirl of fins and teeth.

Sarah turned back to the wall, and began to climb.

On the ledge above, Wyatt was also now pulling her up, hand-over-hand. Sarah kicked up the wall, as he hauled her up like a winch.

Just a couple feet short from the top, she reached the rope, to pull herself over.

And damned if that pesky latch didn't slip again, the very second she let her grip loose. And once again, she started to drop...

... but she was snagged by an adder-fast hand, as Wyatt caught the front of her harness and yanked her up beside him on the ledge.

Sarah blinked, looking back down into the basin. Then Lori was by her side, taking her weight off her leg, pulling them both back from the edge.

Wyatt took her other arm, removing her harness in the manner he might release a horse's bridle or a dog's leash, before he bent down to examine her broken leg. Sarah simply submitted.

"Yep," he said. "Broke across the shin." He looked up. "My boat's a mile hike past the hot-springs," he said. "You want to wait for the chopper?"

Sarah sighed – she wanted nothing more than to be gone from here. A hike through the woods on a broken leg was almost attractive.

But she nodded. "I'll wait for the chopper."

Another hour at most, she decided, and then she could put it all behind her.

Sarah looked back over her shoulder, down the Cauldron's pit.

She could put it *all* behind her, forever.

In less than forty-eight hours since she'd come home to Lake Perdition, anyone who had survived that night twelve years ago, besides Lori and herself, was now gone.

And then there were two.

Sarah glanced at Lori beside her, silent and subdued.

Wyatt pulled out his phone, looking for an ETA on the chopper. It was the pilot that answered.

"What'cha got, Wyatt? We're fueled up and on our way."

Wyatt nodded to Lori and Sarah.

"We've got one more survivor," he said. "And a few more dead people. Then, I guess we can call it a day."

CHAPTER 34

The grisly events went viral.

Ironically, the immediate sentiment nationwide from *way* too many people was that they couldn't *wait* to get right over and see it for themselves.

Asked for comment on camera, Wyatt expressed doubt that simply closing the lake would keep everyone away.

"It didn't *this* time. You can't underestimate how stupid people can be."

Accepting this wisdom, and attempting to get ahead of it, the Idaho Department of Fish and Game acted quickly and simply poisoned the lake.

They did it the day immediately after Wyatt caught the first out-of-stater sneaking-in. Wyatt made an arrangement with the local town cops to report any cars, particularly those with out of state plates, headed out towards the lake.

It was a pretty easy request, actually – the town's sheriff's office was at the far-end of the only road leading out of town, and while it wasn't illegal to *go* that way, Wyatt simply parked at the edge of the restricted area, and blocked the road with his truck.

After the lake was poisoned, there was a corresponding, reflexive viral outrage. The human body count – twenty-five dead, from the first lost hiker to the water-taxi – was deemed insufficient to justify poisoning an entire lake.

The shouting, however, died down quickly – it was, after all, a 'dead-lake', absent of native species, and overrun with invaders – the outcry was over the sanctity of a body of water.

The lake was announced as 'closed indefinitely', pending scientific review.

Indications were, Lake Perdition was going to be a quiet place for a long time.

CHAPTER 35

Wyatt took Lori home after the chopper carted Sarah off from the Cauldron to the hospital. It was just as far to where Wyatt left his boat, but after everything, a hike alone through the woods back to her place was the less appealing.

It was late afternoon by the time they motored up to her old family house, where Lori looked to spend the first night alone in a long time.

In fact, with Sarah on her way to the hospital, that would make her the only living person on the lake, once the sun went down tonight.

Wyatt left his direct number, informing her police would likely be in contact.

Lori watched from the dock as Wyatt backed his boat back out into deeper water, before turning back out into the cove, waving professionally as he left her behind. Lori followed him with her eyes.

He was a better man than she had actually expected him to be.

In retrospect, in the two short days she'd known him, he had, offhand and quite casually, saved both her and Sarah's lives. Granted, he'd done so as he might with livestock, but he still did it.

Lori typed Wyatt's name next to his number, putting him on auto-dial – a handy guy to have on-call.

Her thoughts turned speculative – he would certainly not be her first older man.

Of course, he had not responded to her bikini-flirting, but Lori suspected that was because he was a bit soft on Sarah. That might be more of a problem.

Not that Lori had never been part of a triangle before – just not the *third* corner. She'd been the top corner, even the second corner, and she'd been the other-woman more than once.

She just wasn't sure she could do it, if the other woman was Sarah – who she *still* hadn't called. Her number was now second, just below Wyatt's, on her list of contacts.

But now, as she checked, Lori saw notifications for several other messages as well.

They were numbers she didn't recognize, but the caller-ID indicated her father's law-firm.

Lori tapped her voicemail, set her teeth, bracing for the worst.

Unexpectedly, it was good news.

Not just good – near miraculous considering her circumstance.

The first recorded message, from a man who identified himself as Thomas Collins, Dave Nelson's direct superior, was to inform her that people were asking for her story – and offering large sums of money for it.

Several messages followed, all giving varying names, in different versions of the same voice, professionally personable, exhorting her to call back as soon as possible.

Less than half-a-day ago, Dave was getting exit-papers ready on behalf of these same people.

The proffered sums must be large indeed.

At the moment, Lori was a little too numb from the day to even quite believe it.

Could it be, this tragedy had made her viable again? What kind of monkey's paw, black-serendipity was that?

Not to look a gift-horse in the mouth, but it seemed like accepting payment from the Devil.

Speaking of, there was still that pesky DA's office. But at least, she still had lawyers.

She scrolled through several text-messages left with the voicemails, all from people she had never even talked to before. Someone like Dave always handled it all.

Apparently, Hollywood was actually expressing interest. They had already received a call from a semi-famous documentary filmmaker, named Ashley Wells, who produced a weekly series called *Monster Hunters*.

And this was just based on what happened today. There was also a lot of backstory.

Lori wondered if Sarah would be getting similar calls – the only other living witness. After all, *she* was really at the center of the backstory, not to mention what happened at the Cauldron today.

And *that* was something Lori found nagging at her.

What exactly *did* she see down the Cauldron's basin this afternoon?

Sarah was an adept rock-climber – she'd grown up on these hills. It seemed such a silly mistake that she would tangle her rope on a simple straight-up, hundred-foot ascent.

She had been injured, of course, but...

But... it had looked to Lori, for the life of her, that Sarah had knocked Robbie away.

He had been reaching for the rope, and looked like he was going to make it. And that was *after* she'd fallen on him and knocked him loose in the first place.

Robbie was at the house that night too. Lori had been awakened by the sound of his voice – echoes of half-remembered words.

And then a girl's voice.

"They'll never believe you!"

Danielle?

Or had it been Sarah?

And what exactly did that *mean*?

Assuming she'd really heard those voices at all, and they were not figments of a long-ago dream.

Overhead, the sun was dropping into late afternoon. Soon, it would be growing dark.

The wind would rise, and the Cauldron would start moaning like the wails of the damned – the steam would bubble out of the lake and the cracks in the earth – the bird and animal cries would begin.

And Lori would be all alone – the only person in twenty-five miles – the only human-habitation left on a dead lake.

Except for the house across the cove.

Lori looked across the water, where the house-lights were left-on, standing out in the dimming light, shimmering like ghosts in the shifting mist rising from the lake.

Ghosts of the past.

What had she heard that night?

And what exactly had she seen today?

Lori's face bent into a frown, as an unformed image lurked in the back of her mind, just out of the light – a picture she did not want to see.

CHAPTER 36

When Sarah got out of the hospital the next day, it was Wyatt who took her home.

Home, she thought, using the word deliberately. Her home on the lake.

Her business in town was not quite finished, but she found that her perspective on the place had changed. It no longer felt like an albatross – rather a sanctuary, far, far away, perfect for whenever she wanted to hide out from the world.

Over the next week, she helped oversee the poisoning of the lake.

She had actually pitched Wyatt's suggestion about a piranha-fishing season to the Idaho Fish and Game board, as a less ecologically-destructive solution, and was greeted with a long stare and no comment.

They spread poison for a week, in every cove, including the hot-springs and the Cauldron – anywhere a vent might channel into the underground tunnels.

At Sarah's request, Wyatt arranged for a full Fish and Game crew to help clean-up once the fish carcasses began floating to the surface, by the hundreds.

"We don't want every bear on the mountain coming down for a snack," she said.

Especially true, now that she had decided to relocate back to her old lake-house.

The local Fish and Game office was suddenly short a caretaker, an administrator and science-adviser. Sarah had offered to be all three. It seemed like a natural.

Three weeks ago, she would have never believed it – she never intended to come back.

But somehow it was home again.

Now that everyone else was gone.

She was free.

Of course, according to Wyatt, Lori Pike was rumored to be hosting a film-crew in the coming weeks – a cheesy creature-feature/documentary show. There had, in fact, been a message on her own voicemail, from the producer, extending an offer for an interview – a call Sarah never returned.

She *would*, however, pay attention to the goings-on, and make sure she knew what was being put on the record – both about what happened in recent days, and, of course, the backstory.

Sarah sighed.

The backstory.

If they were really going to be filming documentaries, and the story had any kind of legs, someone was probably going to be looking into that now.

That was not ideal. It was *manageable* – as far as public records, there were no loose ends, and Sarah was confident Lori's own version of events were fairly limited.

She would monitor the situation, and reserve her right to step-in and contribute to the public narrative.

Just to make sure the story remained tailored with all the appropriate nips and tucks.

The truth was not quite the story she had told to Wyatt.

Sarah had not told many deliberate lies in her life – she joked once that she only lied in moments of extreme self-interest.

But she knew enough to mold her story with large elements of the truth. It was easier to picture it when you had to create your own version.

Like, for example, how Danielle had fallen and hit her head.

Sarah remembered that part particularly well, because it had been Sarah, herself, who Danielle confronted with her incriminating sex-video.

She held up her phone, playing it right in Sarah's face.

"Look at your ass in the air," Danielle had said. "I just wanted you to see it before I uploaded it onto the internet. Your first porno."

Sarah had moved to stop her – no deeper than that – she reached for her phone, Danielle struggled briefly – Sarah might have thrown a punch or two.

Danielle went down, knocking her head.

That simple. That easy.

Likewise, it had been Sarah herself who suggested the piranha-pond – extorting Robbie to physically carry Danielle's body.

"I'll tell them it was you," she threatened venomously. "They'll never believe you."

Sarah still remembered spitting out those words – vicious, ruthless – yet, all she felt was desperate fear.

She was seventeen, and she reacted as a kid would, trying to hide the mess.

Impulsive decisions, exacerbated by alcohol.

Things grew exponentially worse when Mr. Pike, arriving home, after traveling all hours, had caught them.

He had seen the splash, and walked up on them just as the fish began to swarm.

"Sarah...?" he said, wide-eyed, looking, unbelieving, into the pond.

Sarah and Robbie both stared back, framed like a pair of deer in the headlights, caught as red-handed as could be.

In the pool, the churning water turned red. Danielle's body began twisting and dancing in the water as if still alive – you could already see the white of stripped bone.

Mr. Pike blinked, stepping back, pulling out his phone.

"I'm calling the police," he said.

Sarah felt a surge of panic.

"No, no, no, Mr. Pike," she began, *"please* don't..."

But then she saw the look in his eyes.

So she pushed him, two-handed, right in the chest.

He staggered backwards and fell into the pond, right into the middle of the churning water.

And although Sarah herself had seen him swimming among them, this time they were already frenzied.

She could hear his initial grunts, and then a desperate, doglike yelp, as he made a lunge for the side of the pond.

Sarah could see the fish had already been *at* him – they opened up his guts, and were *inside* him – in the time it took for him to reach the pool's edge, his legs were eaten to the bone, and his internal organs hollowed out.

The message was just reaching the brain, and he began to fade, his arms flapping to a stop, his head lulling – he began to sink, and the fish moved to his face and arms.

Mr. Pike himself had joked about buying a cow-carcass, just to see if they could strip six-hundred pounds in sixty-seconds.

Sarah guessed Leo Pike weighed in at one-hundred and sixty, or less.

He was mostly gone in half a minute.

Sarah checked her watch.

Start to finish, it all took less than five minutes, from the kitchen to the pond.

Suffice to say, she was likely experiencing some degree of shock. She had already been drinking heavily and, while she would not remember this part later, after they left the two bodies in the pond, she had taken Robbie upstairs, and finished the rest of her bottle.

She really *didn't* remember any of it in the morning. And her scream was real when she found them.

But what was worse, was three weeks later, when the flashback-memories all came flooding back. It had been a dozen years, and those images were never more than an eye-blink away.

Still, you learn to live with things.

After all, it was just two incidents, out of her whole life – one, really, since the second was really part of the other.

Unless you count Robbie out at the Cauldron.

She had to call plausible deniability on that one.

If she could have heard Lori's own thoughts, Sarah would have agreed – it would be silly to think a climber as experienced as herself would tangle her gear, in an emergency, no less. She was hardly incompetent.

On the other hand, Sarah had also learned that there was a certain type of guy who would jump right to the aid of a damsel-in-distress.

She wavered as to whether she thought this trait was endearing, condescending, or just instinctual, but it was there.

Wyatt was clearly one of these, albeit a gruff, grab-you-by-your-drawers version.

But she knew Robbie was too.

Despite all the acrimony, Sarah was almost surprised at how easy it was to make him jump.

Mating-instinct was the one thing that superseded self-preservation across all species.

Too bad for Robbie, Sarah was pretty much over *him*. Frankly, he was just the sort of bad influence her mother always said. It was good to be rid of him.

It was a conscious decision.

She wasn't a kid anymore. Today had not been panic. It was necessity – cleaning it all up.

Even any pesky threads that might have been left with Kenny and Deb were now gone.

Sarah could get on with her life in peace.

Of course, there was still Lori. And Wyatt.

Sarah had always felt responsibility for Lori's situation – and despite what Deb tried to tell her, it was not misplaced at all – Sarah knew she had every reason to bear a legitimate burden.

So she would continue to keep her eye on Lori, and do her best to look after her.

And as far as the public went, it was also important to make sure their narratives remained consistent.

Then there was Wyatt.

Sarah had watched him closely in the days following the Cauldron incident.

When he had pulled her up that day, there was a moment where she thought he suspected – that he had seen her knock Robbie from the rope.

Perhaps it was his authority, but after he'd pulled her out of the Cauldron that day, she actually *had* felt a moment of the old panic – and that similar impulse to just push him over the edge and be done – to be *safe*.

It was an unthinking, instinctive response – a fear-reflex, not necessity or anger – just cold, naked panic at being *caught* – finally found out after all this time.

But then he turned and she had seen his eyes – the grim, stony facade actually showed concern – he was grateful she was alive.

That was enough. The panic-impulse passed.

But that was how easy it got.

Standing there, in the moment, she felt a shiver of relief that she had not done it.

In the time since, Wyatt had checked-in on her periodically, always official business, always calling her *ma'am*.

A better man than she expected.

She might actually give him a call, *off* the clock, once she was confident certain secrets were safely buried.

Sarah stood out on her dock, overlooking her lagoon, watching the sun dip over the western hill. She felt the temperature instantly begin to drop.

Across the cove, the Pike-property's automatic lights clicked on.

Sarah knew Lori was home, but no music played.

Lori still had never called.

Sarah eyed the house speculatively. After a moment, she pulled out her phone and tapped-up Lori's number.

She paused, considering.

Then she put the phone back in her pocket and went back inside. She shut the window and closed the curtains.

As the sun set on the lake, the eldritch mist began to rise.

And near the bank of Sarah's lagoon, there came a sudden hiccup of steam, as a bubble broke through the surface, right among the lilies. There was a guttural belch and a glut of geothermal-heated water was released right among the stalks, which were still gummed in egg-jelly – some of them perhaps still viable.

On the surface, the lily pads bubbled, as the water gurgled like a bullfrog, burping-up from below.

CHAPTER 37

The next morning, a hundred miles to the south, standing in rapids that bled onto the Snake River, a fisherman named Carter Wilson was getting his first bite of the day.

This was usually his secret patch – the one he hiked two-miles off-road to fish, because it was always stocked with fat, untouched trout.

Today, however, he'd gotten nothing but broken line. He was on his fifth leader. Something was making short work of his tackle.

He had switched from bait to a lure, when he got his first identifiable bite of the day.

Carter smiled, recognizing the signature-hit of a large trout. He yanked the line sure, then began to reel it in.

Suddenly, the line went alive, jerking in all directions.

Carter spun the reel as fast as he could, but even as he yanked his catch clear of the water, he felt the load had gone light.

Dangling from the end of the line was the head of a large trout.

Carter looked around the water, and saw several darting shapes disappearing into the cracks.

He held up the fish's head and ran his finger along a series of circular bites, several of them bigger than a quarter.

"What the hell did *this*?" he said aloud, looking nervously at the water around him.

He jumped as his phone suddenly chimed in his pocket – his wife's ringtone – a message beeped.

"*Are they biting?*"

THE END

CHECK OUT OTHER GREAT DEEP SEA THRILLERS

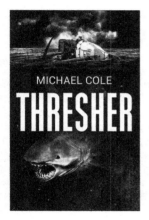

THRESHER
by **Michael Cole**

In the aftermath of a hurricane, a series of strange events plague the coastal waters off Florida. People go into the water and never return. Corpses of killer whales drift ashore, ravaged from enormous bite marks. A fishing trawler is found adrift, with a mysterious gash in its hull.

Transferred to the coastal town of Merit, police officer Leonard Riker uncovers the horrible reality of an enormous Thresher shark lurking off the coast. Forty feet in length, it has taken a territorial claim to the waters near the town harbor. Armed with three-inch teeth, a scythe-like caudal fin, and unmatched aggression, the beast seeks to kill anything sharing the waters.

THE GUILLOTINE
by **Lucas Pederson**

1,000 feet under the surface, Prehistoric Anthropologist, Ash Barrington, and his team are in the midst of a great archeological dig at the bottom of Lake Superior where they find a treasure trove of bones. Bones of dinosaurs that aren't supposed to be in this particular region. In their underwater facility, Infinity Moon, Ash and his team soon discover a series of underground tunnels. Upon exploring, they accidentally open an ice pocket, thawing the prehistoric creature trapped inside. Soon they are being attacked, the facility falling apart around them, by what Ash knows is a dunkleosteus and all those bones were from its prey. Now...Ash and his team are the prey and the creature will stop at nothing to get to them.

Check out other great

Sea Monster Novels!

Michael Cole

CREATURE OF LAKE SHADOW

It was supposed to be a simple bank robbery. Quick. Clean. Efficient. It was none of those. With police searching for them across the state, a band of criminals hide out in a desolate cabin on the frozen shore of Lake Shadow. Isolated, shrouded in thick forest, and haunted by a mysterious history, they thought it was the perfect place to hide. Tensions mount as they hear strange noises outside. Slain animals are found in the snow. Before long, they realize something is watching them. Something hungry, violent, and not of this world. In their attempt to escape, they found the Creature of Lake Shadow.

Matt James

SUB-ZERO

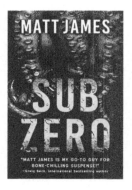

The only thing colder than the Antarctic air is the icy chill of death... Off the coast of McMurdo Station, in the frigid waters of the Southern Ocean, a new species of Antarctic octopus is unintentionally discovered. Specialists aboard a state-of-the-art DARPA research vessel aim to apply the animal's "sub-zero venom" to one of their projects: An experimental painkiller designed for soldiers on the front lines. All is going according to plan until the ship is caught in an intense storm. The retrofitted tanker is rocked, and the onboard laboratory is destroyed. Amid the chaos, the lead scientist is infected by a strange virus while conducting the specimen's dissection. The scientist didn't die in the accident. He changed.

CHECK OUT OTHER GREAT
DEEP SEA THRILLERS

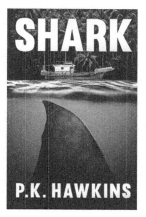

SHARK: INFESTED WATERS
by P.K. Hawkins

For Simon, the trip was supposed to be a once in a lifetime gift: a journey to the Amazon River Basin, the land that he had dreamed about visiting since he was a child. His enthusiasm for the trip may be tempered by the poor conditions of the boat and their captain leading the tour, but most of the tourists think they can look the other way on it. Except things go wrong quickly. After a horrific accident, Simon and the other tourists find themselves trapped on a tiny island in the middle of the river. It's the rainy season, and the river is rising. The island is surrounded by hungry bull sharks that won't let them swim away. And worst of all, the sharks might not be the only blood-thirsty killers among them. It was supposed to be the trip of a lifetime. Instead, they'll be lucky if they make it out with their lives at all.

DARK WATERS
by Lucas Pederson

Jörmungandr is an ancient Norse sea monster. Thought to be purely a myth until a battleship is torn a part by one.

With his brother on that ship, former Navy Seal and deep-sea diver, Miles Raine, sets out on a personal vendetta against the creature and hopefully save his brother. Bringing with him his old Seal team, the Dagger Points, they embark on a mission that might very well be their last.

But what happens when the hunters become the hunted and the dark waters reveal more than a monster?

Made in the USA
Middletown, DE
11 November 2022